C000263498

The
TWO
WOMEN
of
AGANATZ

To my father
Frank Golden
1912-1993

This book is dedicated to the memory of my father who spent the war years 1941-43 in North Africa and instilled in me a desire to witness the landscape of the desert at first hand.

The TWO WOMEN of AGANATZ

FRANK GOLDEN

WOLFHOUND PRESS

First published 1994 by
WOLFHOUND PRESS Ltd
68 Mountjoy Square
Dublin 1

and Wolfhound Press (UK)
18 Coleswood Rd
Harpenden, Herts AL5 1EQ

© Frank Golden 1994

All rights reserved. No part of this book may be reproduced or utilised in any form or by any means electronic or mechanical including photography, filming, recording, video recording, photocopying, or by any information storage and retrieval system or shall not, by way of trade or otherwise, be lent, resold or otherwise circulated in any form of binding or cover other than that in which it is published without prior permission in writing from the publisher. The moral rights of the author have been asserted.

This book is fiction. All characters, incidents and names have no connection with any persons living or dead. Any apparent resemblance is purely coincidental.

Wolfhound Press receives financial assistance from the Arts Council/An Chomhairle Ealaíon, Dublin.

British Library Cataloguing in Publication Data
A catalogue record for this book is available from the British Library.
ISBN 0 86327 393 3

Thanks to the Silver Siren for using her exquisite mind towards the betterment of this work, and for her friendship.
To PEL, first reader and old friend.
To Margaret, for the Tigín years, during which much of this book was written.
To Mark, Trish, Ray, Keith and Miranda for their friendship and support.
To Maria for her warmth and love.
To my daughter Eve, for her love.
To my family, for their support.
My thanks also to Bernard and Mary Loughlin, for their hospitality, during my residencies at the Tyrone Guthrie Centre, Annaghmakerrig, Co Monaghan, where some of this book was written.
Acknowledgement to *Illuminations* edited by Peter McMillan where some sections of this book first appeared.
I also wish to acknowledge the support of the Arts Council of Ireland from whom I received a Bursary in Literature 1993.

Typesetting: Wolfhound Press
Cover illustration: Keith Payne / Cover design: Joe Gervin
Printed in the Republic of Ireland by Colour Books, Dublin

Part I

Liano was born to Olan in the spring, seven months after Eighad's disappearance. The rains came early that year and the dormant seeds which had lain in the sands for decades uncurled through the crust of compacted sand and stone, festooning the floor of the desert with flowers. It had been the first spring in years when the rains had been sufficient to goad and bolster such extraordinary growth. Olan had found in this exceptional spring a note of encouragement, as though the desert had conjoined with her in celebrating this surge and renewal of life.

The birthing had been simple with the child easing out like a slick seed from its casing. Olan had bitten through the cord with a primitive sense of propriety, crying tears of resilience and self-congratulation. She had no doubts about her ability to cradle, rear and safeguard this infant. It was hers, hers alone, and holding the child aloft she recommended it to the wind and to the flourishing earth. This after all was her zone of the desert, her environ of earth and no one would tamper with her possessions. She brought the child over her heart and they lay together on the wool carpet until dawn.

Olan had prepared a room for the newborn long in advance. According to tradition the chamber had been sealed off from the effects of natural light by a series of silk veils of varying densities. These veils approximated the uterine environment in which the child had existed for so long and each day following the birth saw one of them removed.

Mother and child blossomed during those first months. Nurturing the baby had unexpectedly helped Olan to reclaim her own body. No longer distended she swayed and loped in the lush garden of the Fortress like some stupendous sleek animal.

The garden, which in its size and confusion of paths more resembled a jungle, seemed to echo through its flowerings and generations of seed the robust zeal which had forwarded the child. In apparent communion with Olan the garden became guardian to her needs, a bountiful and extravagant parcel of ground providing them with all they needed to survive.

On clear days when the sharpness of the light highlighted the nuances of sand formations near the great rock of Bradaz, Olan would strap the child to her middle and herd her small flock of sheep to areas far removed from the Fortress. Walking with bare feet on carpets of lavender and dhua moss she would sing gently in a tone which the desert held and returned. The openness of the desert instilled a calm, its gifts of silence and distance counterpointing the intensity of the garden, allowing her own nature to expand accordingly.

On nights when the moon was up and they had travelled a good distance from Aganatz, Olan lay with Liano underneath the stars reciting a litany of names — names of animals and plants which inhabited her kingdom, things which had threaded themselves into the matrix of her mind and body. She blessed the motivated land and laid her hands over it in a gesture which inferred a magical bond. In much the same way as she stroked and kissed her own child, she soothed the terrific labours of the sand, weaving her hands within its folds, solacing its centre.

With Liano she lay under a broad coverlet of cloth and like semaphores they communicated with that rare earth. This was Olan invested in the scented darkness, holding up the delivered fruit of her womb, draping the child with flowers and leaves in a pattern traced from the great circle stones at Bradaz.

From the beginning Olan adored the child, devouring every minute with her. She felt each suck of milk layer her presence in Liano. She conceived of the process as a gradual accretion of influences which would bind them irrevocably together. They would have recourse to each other, be for each other a sympathetic reference, their love would stimulate the kind of bond which had always been denied her.

There would be nothing haphazard about this child. Olan would foster love and obedience to her will. It would be like the fabrication of a profound enchantment. She would compose her work according to her vision of fidelity and devotion and she would abide in the presence of her creation. The child would become for Olan a tabernacle of succour. The child's purity would be a thing contained and never brutalised, never mutilated, a purity which would be encased like a great prize or jewel, to be witnessed and enjoyed only by Olan.

After years of what Olan termed outrageous degradation at the hands of Eighad she felt the need to invent a life according to her own dictates. For this and other reasons she attempted to deny Eighad's content in the child. She even managed to confuse his part in her. Perhaps there had been no seed. She was prepared to work on this idea and ultimately to deny that it had been his rod which had forced her womb to fruit. She laboured over a solution which revolved around the exceptional advantage of her sex: an inverted penis she argued, burdened her inner wall.

Mother and child were the only inhabitants within the cavernous structure of Aganatz. The outside world, as Olan deemed it, did not trespass on this domain. Those few who tried to gain entrance were held at bay like wolves at the torch's end. Because of its isolation and the storied horrors which were meant to possess it, travellers and merchants alike refused to break the seal of its circumference. No one came to bang against the bolted gates beyond which woman and child were occasionally glimpsed from a distance, their heads covered as they herded their sheep.

In later years Olan explained this to Liano.

'They're afraid. Afraid to beg for water. Afraid to steal our fruit. They believe that everything we touch or walk on is thereafter poisoned and corrupt. Amongst themselves they talk of our curses dripping like snake's piss on their heads. If a caravan comes by this route on its way south they manoeuvre around the perimeter reciting prayers which they believe shard our spirits. They keep their children's eyes shielded, their own foreheads painted with tattoos. No one wants to breathe the same air as us. We are degenerate forms, evil corroborations linked to the devil. If they have to set up camp near us they burn pyres of incense. You can smell it from the battlements and hear the chant of their vigil as they try to protect their children who are kept awake lest the chimeras and ghosts which emanate from us creep through their ears and yawning mouths.'

Olan did everything she could to reinforce these beliefs among the travellers so that both she and her daughter remained undisturbed. They had become and would remain remote entities on the edge of a world in which no one was particularly interested. It was Olan's determined wish to subsist in her own chasm of feeling and to secure this she had to establish for herself and her child an almost alien status in that landscape. It was an insularity which if anything had become more desired after Eighad's disappearance, an insularity which now admitted the revolution of only one other, her daughter.

For years after Liano's birth no one came near them. They remained fastened in their oasis, living in its melted centre, becoming part of the garden which grew up around them. A garden which as the years passed seemed to become intimately linked to Olan's inner life, to the extent that flowers favoured by her would respond spontaneously to her touch..

Each day mother and child laboured in a different part of the garden, whether in the date grove which occupied a large area by the northern turret, in the vegetable plot to the south or among the tamarisk, frankincense and ilb trees which grew over a sloping area in the western quarter.

In temperament the child was cool, a little retreated and without the natural exuberance and beauty which described her mother. Olan sometimes found Liano to be lacking in the kind of sensual over-abundance with which she had expected a child of hers to be gifted. None of this she believed was irremedial.

Liano was lean and sinewy and seemed to embody a rationality which was alien to her mother. But surely, Olan thought, the longer they abided with each other the more likely it was that they would achieve a similitudinous state of harmony. Liano would come to reflect Olan's unities and the unities of the natural world which surrounded her.

According to her continuing vision of her daughter, Olan attempted to instill in her an understanding of the ritual nature of certain actions and demonstrated rites which had to be carried out in conjunction with natural cycles and patterns. Liano's antipathy to this area of knowledge was marked and it was during this period that Olan first began to harbour doubts as to their compatibility. It wasn't that the child did not love her or want to be with her but there was a distance in her, a desire from her earliest years to move into the unchartered spaces beyond the Fortress.

At every opportunity Liano roamed in the desert with her tiny pet dog Mola trailing behind her. Olan would see them scampering among the low ridge of dunes which surrounded the Fortress, running after the great lizards which stood like sentinels above their holes, warming themselves in the midday heat.

When she was five Liano asked her mother if she could have a lizard of her own. Olan agreed and provided Liano with some timber to construct a cage. For weeks during the latter end of that summer Liano worked on the construction of the cage. When it was finally uncovered Olan could not disguise her surprise. It was an elaborate structure almost fifteen feet long with dropped levels, cantilever movements and tunnels made of braided leaves. Olan applauded her daughter's industry while privately finding the precociousness of the design vaguely unsettling. She had no choice now but to go in search of one of the great taubs and bring it back.

Finally one of the lizards was captured. Liano was ecstatic. It was the culmination of a childish need to possess something that was her own, but strangely it provoked a feeling of jealousy in Olan which she tried to dissemble.

Liano became completely absorbed in the habits and functions of the lizard which she called Amman. She doted on it, feeding it the best morsels of food, talking to it, but never trying to coax it to settle in her lap or attempting to touch it. She was content for the most part simply to observe it.

It was the nature of her almost delinquent attention to the lizard's functions which began to disturb Olan. It seemed to her that her daughter's features were beginning to manage themselves towards a mirroring of those of the lizard. Her tongue appeared elongated and sticky, darting like a streamlined organ against her food. Her movements became contained, her limbs coiled on springs, her spirit soiled and orientated to that of the reptile.

After some weeks of captivity, however, the lizard began to fail. It would lie for hours at a time in one corner of the cage its whole aspect exuding a sense of defeat and mourning. The creature was close to death before Liano decided to relinquish her hold on it.

Early one morning she placed Amman in a woollen sack and ventured out into the desert. Knowing there was a colony of great taubs to the east of the Fortress she made for it and in brilliant sunshine allowed her beautiful lizard to move onto the currents of sand fanned out before them. The lizard looked startled for a moment then suddenly his senses picked up, the tone of his skin seemed to lose its pallor and his eyes to regain a hint of their old life. There was a perceptible inflection of suspicion as he doubted the fact of his imminent release. Testing the terms of his bondage he gave Liano a last look and scuttled off to a distant ridge.

For years afterwards Liano looked for him and occasionally believed she recognised him with his feet curled up off the desert floor, his head prodded to the sky, an elevated master of his zone, a creature whose intimate range she knew and now identified with, a creature whose secret of adaption to this barren landscape she believed had been divined and whose reflected spirit would ward her in the years ahead.

When Liano was seven an incident occurred which was to create a rift between mother and daughter, an incident which stirred memories of a past Olan had rigorously sought to deny.

Of the four towers which were part of the structure of Aganatz, the northern one had from Liano's earliest memories always been locked. She had asked her mother on a number of occasions whether she could see inside but access was consistently denied. Olan maintained that it held the detritus of years past; it was a storeroom, she said, of spent objects, things which had lost their value but which could not be thrown away. Although accepting the explanation Liano still wanted to see inside.

Her opportunity came in the winter of that year. She was in the small timber hut constructed in a clearing which they used for compressing dates into compacted blocks. In the far corner of the hut was a vat of fermented date juice, to the right the light caught the glimmer of a jumble of keys under some rags of soiled cloth. She examined them, figuring immediately that the largest might open the arched door of the northern turret. Determined to follow her hunch she decided to go to the turret when her mother next went beyond the Fortress walls.

Five days later Liano stood on the western battlements watching her mother move off. It was only when she perceived her as a small dot that she went to the tower. With Mola by her side she ran by the giant blago trees which curved in a dense canopy over the pathway parallel to the north section of the Fortress. The door itself was covered in a tangle of ivies and myrtles. These she stripped back, their root suckers leaving scar lines on the wood. Turning the key in the lock the heavy tower door creaked inwards. In the half-light she could see a spiral staircase lead upwards to a landing on the first floor. The stairs were dank and musty with filaments of webs and clumps of moss growing from between the morticed blocks of stone.

Liano placed her hand on the wooden handle of the first floor chamber door and pushed. This too was locked. Breathing deeply she settled herself, pushed the third key into the lock, forced it slightly and heard it tumble. As the door swung inwards she stepped back.

Warily she went within the sanctum around which the aroma of intrigue seemed manifest in every mote of dust. Illuminated by a shaft of sunlight which came through the large window on her right were a series of enormous paintings covering the circular walls of the chamber. The paintings were abstract in form with lines merging over and above particular geometric shapes. Liano felt an immediate sense of connectedness to these works. For the first time she felt that this was a territory of stone which spelt home. Although she could not articulate it, the essence of her own being seemed to be registered in the room. Beneath a number of the scrolled paintings was a name which Liano tried to make out. Once deciphered she pronounced it aloud. The name uttered was that of Eighad and her spine shivered as the syllables rolled like a wave-echo in the room.

Against the far wall was a large bed with a woven rug draped over it. She shook the dust off and sat down continuing to feast her eyes on the circular weave of images which surrounded her. She lay back and slept. It was only the sound of the entrance gates being opened which woke her. Rushing out of the room she closed the door and scrambled down the stairs. She could hear Mola barking in excitement at her mother's return. Locking the tower door she replaced the keys and ran to greet her.

From that day on, the experience of the room possessed her. She retained in her memory images of the paintings and deemed them as precious as the rag doll Olan had once made for her. The room was something her mother wanted nothing to do with, so surely, she reasoned, it could be hers. A place of retreat, a hiding place where no one else could enter. The name of Eighad also obsessed her and she wanted Olan to offer up her memories.

In the months that followed, Liano went to the room whenever her mother's absence permitted. Olan had noticed in her daughter an air of detachment or self-absorption and asked if anything was the matter. The issue was always avoided but a staleness of contained secrets on both sides began to interject themselves and acted as a buffer between the two.

During these visits to Eighad's room Liano sat surrounded by the circular current of colour which merged over time into one continuous piece. In her meticulous way she uncovered various artifacts belonging to Eighad. These included books, clothes, painting materials and, hidden in the bottom of a large trunk, some notebooks. The notebooks existed as a key to the possible elaboration of the character of Eighad; yet now that she had them in her possession she was in no hurry to read them, feeling that they might reverse or taint her already fixed view of this vanished personality.

Little by little Liano brought oddments from the chamber back to her room and hid them. Sometimes tiny sketches or medals until she had an assortment of mementoes sequestered and deftly concealed.

It was in the winter of that year when Olan, browsing through her daughter's bedroom, discovered these relics of Eighad's arranged like jewels in a small timber box. Unable at first to credit what her daughter had done she denied the reality of the situation and questioned whether in fact her own memory wasn't in default. Had she perhaps placed these objects here herself?

During this period Olan experienced a profound sense of betrayal, a feeling that Liano had in fact intuited her need to excise Eighad from her memory but to spite her had dragged his spirit back and allowed it to occupy a central position in their lives.

Olan said nothing to Liano but lapsed into a period of depression and for days refused to come out of her room. Languishing in darkness she realised that the spirit of Eighad roved in Liano, that his sickness was part of her, his flesh part of the child's corruption; it could not be otherwise. In the face of all her actions and attentions, Olan believed that he had managed to regenerate and sustain himself in her child. Details of Liano's first seven years emphasising her kinship with her father were retrieved from memory. Olan felt that the unguarded warmth and affection she had displayed up to then could now no longer be offered.

Years later when the topic of Eighad posed less of a threat, Liano understood that her mother's memory of him was so fractured that the truth of their relationship could never be distilled. Olan's memories of him, disclosed in the years that followed, were various, with the only common factor being the bitterness with which her mother described them.

'When he came to Aganatz he was a mere child, a barbarous entity who covered the walls of his room with his own waste. He hung from the grooves and limbs of trees like a mad animal, ripping songbirds with his teeth, discarding their bodies in the water, corrupting everything he laid his foul hands on. You could hear him in the night moving on all fours, his eyes luminous like tetras, his tongue scraping the walls by my window, crunching night beetles and spiders, his lightning quick fingers snatching bats from the air, his fanged teeth shredding the corded rope which fastened the frame doorway to my bedroom.'

'Eighad was a formulation of the desert, a mistake ordained by my own stupidity. I laid four sections of an oval mirror in the sand according to an ancient pattern creating two isosceles and two right-angled triangles on the perimeter of my zone. A fifth section reflected upwards towards the sky. This organisation was meant to betray the essence of a spirit I could tame and the burning sun to incorporate it forever in the fifth section of glass. All of this would have added to my power. However in contravention of transcendent laws, the spirit of Eighad floundered into this arena, his physical life was returned and against all expectations I had no dominion over him.'

'I had no choice but to take him in. He was weak, brutalised by the desert, forlorn and deranged by his lack of food and water. I had no choice I tell you. He was a pitiful specimen, one which I restored and sheltered. He recovered well and even came to feel that he would like to remain. Of course I said yes. I was in love. He said he loved me but I knew I was never enough for him. He began to batten me down, to bleed me and work his lusts roughly inside me. He needled an intricate linkage of hatreds up my anus. He extracted the mallow of my love and mashed it between his hands. He left for days at a time, escaping me. It got to the point where it was more than he could stand to spend a week in my presence. During the great storm of our seventh year he crept beyond the outer limits of the Fortress. I never saw him again but heard from a traveller that he made it to Doan where he now lives with a whore from the Jabodin tribe.'

On and on they went, a compendium of dreams, memories and hallucinations, a powdery selection of images which once they were blown away left the faint smell of some foul combustion in the nostrils. Liano tried to correct or interrogate Olan's view of Eighad but it was like trying to construct a solid object from amorphous units. In the end she did not seek a consistent fiction but settled for her own image.

The problem for Liano was that her sense of things was not comparative. She had no alternative life with which to compare hers, no system of values to intercede against those offered up by Olan. She sometimes felt like her mother's version of herself under the ruling thumb of Eighad, an object used, brutalised and then discarded. She was compromised by her lack of knowledge, her isolation, and by the fact that Olan no longer trusted her.

In the early mornings Liano often sat above the vaulted gates of the main entrance listening to lime-crested birds organise a melody among the trees. She pieced together sections from her mother's fabled past, incidents which she used as a basis for what she wanted for herself.

— ~ —

As the years of Liano's childhood passed, mother and daughter gradually grew more independent of each other. At a certain point Liano understood that a percentage of her mother was denied her, that her bond was one which led them to identify their differences. Occasionally there were months when their relationship warmed, rekindling memories of those first doting years, but that temporarily recessed memory describing injury would always resurface, making one or the other back off.

At such times Liano retreated to the desert where she felt free of the complex bonds which tied her to Olan, free also of the garden which, although lush and bountiful, pressed against her, its loud and clamorous greenery making her feel like a prisoner. The garden was mutable, the desert obstinate and fixed with a purity and simplicity which appealed to her. There were so few things in that zone to be named and she was intimate with everything which survived.

Most of the time Liano felt like a casual element in her mother's life, a child whose ability to please or to appease made her see herself as a corrosive factor, a thing which her mother had of necessity to place at arm's length in order to preserve herself. Feeling rejected, shunned, she would journey for days at a time into the desert often making for a spot she called Obluda, a hiding place from which she observed the caravans on their way south. The spectacle of camels and pack mules stretching in sinewy lines with men, women and children following behind, often led her to dream of going with them, of slipping in unnoticed among them, of visiting towns and settlements beyond the southern tip of the desert. Her mother's warnings, however, rang in her head and she always balked at taking such a step.

Throughout her childhood Liano experienced the periodic warp of Olan's mind. It was like a seasonal outbreak of aberrant gestures and actions. The duration and cause varied, but Olan's unpredictability and unmanageableness during such bouts both threatened and intimidated the child.

Alone in the southern quarter of the garden she saw the mould of her mother's physical presence alter like a piece of hot metal. There was a sense that from her head ranged tentacles and from her arms bristling hairs like thorns. Olan's eyes seemed focused on the course of some internal vision. Liano was too frightened to help and could only listen as her mother incanted her prayers and picked up stone after stone, beating them to a blood rhythm. At the height of these turns Liano would glimpse her mother running naked through the undergrowth, screaming wildly, ranting her tongue, raving her arms in the seamless night, trying to manage her chaos.

There was no one to help Liano at such times, so she invoked the name of Eighad, ascribing to him a kind of omnipotence. The movement of terror would end and when it did her mother would lie exhausted in some part of the garden, asking to be taken to her bed and for the shutters to be drawn.

Liano would watch all night as her mother worked like some strenuous beast, flailing against illusions which seemed to surround her.

Days later when Olan moved again in the garden, animals and birds would weave patterns around her, appraising her difference.

Sometimes her mother lay among the reeds and lily pads of the pond, her startling body appearing to section the water into cubes. She floated like a huge olive fish, her arms outstretched, her legs opened, her nipples leaving trace lines of their own in the water. Liano watched her mother create these ordained patterns over and over while petals and crushed leaves were scattered from a porcelain bowl which rested on her floating stomach. Olan's fingers smelt of aloe for days after. As she swam, the water discoloured and from between her legs a line of blood fanned out before her.

When Liano was eleven she asked her mother why this was. Lifting her dress Olan explained it as a sign.

'Here,' she said. 'Put your finger inside.'

Liano was reluctant to do so but then gently moved her index finger up between the parted sides of her mother's vagina. Her finger felt fluid in the blood filled cavity and Liano pulled it out quickly.

Olan said, 'This is a sign we will share.'

From then on Liano waited, checking her body regularly, always expecting her removed finger to be stained with a spot of blood. When it finally happened she was not aware of it. Sitting up one morning there was a sudden flow of blood which dribbled down her leg when she stood. She ran to Olan who was in the garden, a palm full of clotted blood in her fist.

Olan calmed her down and went to get a bottle of oleander scented oil which, after she had undressed her, she spread over Liano's body. They went down to the pool together. Olan waded with Liano through a surface swarm of dragon flies feeding on the larva of siva bugs. Eels which infested the pond rose from the bottom and wriggled beneath the surface. As Liano floated she could feel them nibble the hairs on the underside of her back.

'I'll hold you up,' said Olan. 'The eels won't hurt you.'

Supporting her with one hand she stroked Liano's navel with the other.

When Liano stepped out of the pond the blood which had issued from her remained contained by a film of oil. The disc of blood floated on the surface and Liano imagined spindly insects working away on its underside. She waited for it to scramble out of the water and run after her.

That night Olan came to her daughter's room for the first time in many years.

Olan could see that she'd been crying.

Liano described the pain.

'It feels like a hot stone that's getting bigger and bigger.'

Olan brushed Liano's fringe away from her face and told her she would feel better soon.

As they lay together Liano felt warm and safe. She was reassured by her mother's presence, believing that when she needed her most, Olan was there for her.

Olan said little but stroked her daughter's hair and whispered gently into her ear. Desert moonlight flooded in through the high window of the bedroom spreading slants of yellow light on the stone floor. Olan snuggled closer to her daughter saying, 'Liano. Perhaps I should check, just to make sure everything's alright.'

Liano wasn't sure what she meant but when her mother's fingers moved between her legs, she said nothing.

The first thing which occurred to her was that she had done the same to her mother. Still there was something which made her feel uneasy, a voice inside her which said, '*This is not right*'.

Olan gently moved her thumb over Liano's clitoris and began to masturbate her.

'What are you doing, mother?'

'It's only something to help the pain. It will make it go away more quickly.'

A shudder ran through Liano and her spine tingled. She felt strange and wanted her mother both to stop and not to stop. She felt confused. When she touched her mother's hand Olan withdrew her fingers.

When asked how she felt Liano admitted that the pain didn't feel so bad, but she wanted to cry.

Shortly after that Liano fell asleep. When she awoke Olan was gone. In her place nestled Mola, an unsatisfactory replacement, a comfort rag which offered only the barest physical reassurance, a creature which, for all its loyalty, only seemed to emphasize her loneliness. There was something in what had occurred that night which troubled Liano deeply. She blamed herself. If she hadn't bled, then wasn't it true that her mother wouldn't have had to check? Maybe everything wasn't alright. Maybe there really was something wrong with her and Olan was afraid to tell her.

For nights after that Liano expected her mother to return. She never did. It was months later when Liano was awoken by a movement in the undergrowth beneath her window. She saw the glow of a candle gradually illuminate the darkness. When the door of her bedroom opened Liano was struck by her mother's appearance.

Olan was dressed in a long white nightgown, her face stripped with henna and kohl, her eyelids deeply shaded in blue. She looked beautiful, her hair hanging loose and swinging down past the curve of her back. She smiled at Liano, then blew out the candle. She said nothing but crawled in beside Liano kissing her gently on the cheek.

Liano was tense, nervous, and the smell of her mother made her feel nauseous. She wanted to blurt out so many things but Olan, with a commanding gesture, placed her finger over her mouth and kissed her forehead. She could feel her mother's naked body beside her own.

She threw her arms around Olan and began to cry. Olan held her tight for a moment then levered her away.

Stretching Liano's arms back behind her head she took a small pouch from around her neck and began to anoint her with red oil. After making a series of cruciform, oval and wave patterns on her daughter's body, she wrote the name of Eighad on her belly.

Olan became more intense, swarming herself over the child, twining her legs around her, kissing her tiny breasts, kissing her lips, tonguing between her legs, finally making her do the same to her. It felt strange, but Liano did it. In one way she felt closer to her mother now, closer than she had ever been. She didn't want to lose that.

At some point in the course of the night Olan placed a curved stone in her daughter's hand. The stone had been warmed and she said to Liano, 'Put it between my legs.' Olan maintained her own rhythm with the stone inside her, increasing in passion until her body seemed like a constant vibration at the ends of Liano's fingers. Finally she uttered an animal-like squeal and lay back relaxed.

When these manoeuvres were over Liano was shocked by her mother's indifference. Olan left her feeling resentful and angry without being able to articulate why. She lay in the darkness for hours crying, trying to understand her mother's actions, rubbing with her own tears the signs which dressed her body, believing in the end that it was her fault, that there was something wrong with her which made her mother act in this way.

In the years that followed, Olan's visits became a regular feature in her daughter's life. Liano came to terms with the nature of these actions in so far as she became manipulative in her own right. She began to see it as part of an inevitable, an inscrutable momentum, a movement of energy which was occasionally positive in that it was a point of physical contact, a sapping of the possible violences which would have been elaborated without that pressure of flesh.

Both came to appreciate their bodies as units of power, their sexuality as a contrivance, an arena in which the struggle for dominion was played out, with the order of their brutalizing actions becoming a complex game, a fluctuating state of subservience.

By her late teens Liano had the upper hand.

— ~ —

One late summer evening, nineteen years after her birth, Liano stood under the lintel of her mother's doorway and looked at her seated before the open window at the far end of the room. Olan's face was half-mirrored in a section of hanging glass. She appeared pre-occupied. In her hand she held a carved ivory comb. The desert air filled the room with the smell of dying uaba blossoms. The mealiness of the smell made Liano pucker her nose and turn her head slightly to the left.

Walking towards Olan, she had the sudden vision of her mother's flesh as a compost of dead matter with maturing bulbs buried in its layers, of weeds and flowers rooted in her pores, of a system of life dying back into her body and then regenerating. She saw it as a host for parasitic seeds and insects which swam in her sweat and multiplied between her toes.

Standing behind her, this visionary subcurrent of organic growth vanished. Once again her mother's skin appeared mesmerically smooth and unblemished. So unlike her own. Liano felt momentarily discouraged. Taking the comb she ran it briskly through lengths of Olan's hair, occasionally allowing the tips of her fingers to light on her scalp, giving it a turgid scratch.

Drawing the woollen robe off her shoulders Liano began to massage Olan's neck rotating down to her shoulders, pressurising key points with her thumbs. Olan's head keeled over as though broken, lolling to the front, then to either side, as the tension flowed out. This nightly ritual which had originated as delinquent foreplay, was now offered as an indulgence, an action or consideration which Liano could not as yet conceive of terminating.

Leaving the comb to one side for a moment, Liano lit the oil lamp by the window. The flare of light illuminated Olan's face giving it a mellow warmth. Again Liano was struck by her mother's beauty. Tonight she saw her as a voluptuary, a glowing body of faceted sensuality. She envied her. With her thumb she traced the elegant jawline down to the chin. Its purity seemed to singe the hardened tips of her fingers. A sneer briefly marred her own features. Given the bias of Olan's physicality, Liano's disgruntlement and envy seemed inevitable. It was an injustice which gnawed like a mole at the pit of her stomach, making her want to vomit.

Liano had never grown used to the disparity in their physical presences. Olan, when she was feeling indulgent explained her daughter's occasionally harrowing image as a phase, something which would pass, leaving in its wake a memorable beauty, not unlike her own. For Liano, these statements always contained an air of unreality, a fantasist's projection of the ideal. They were nothing more than a comforting sequence of words with the belied truth eventually surfacing for air. She heard it now ring in her ears.

'You will never be as beautiful as me.'

Taking a long wire brush Liano began again to comb Olan's hair, drawing lengths of it over her forearm and brushing through it. Looking out the window to the mesh of stars trailing beyond the eastern turret, she caught sight of herself in the twirling shard of glass hanging in front of her mother. She felt a sudden wave of revulsion at the sight of her own face.

Her hair was short, lank and hung in bangs down her forehead and over her eyes. Her skin was marked by pimples and scabs with small craters in her cheeks betraying the damage of frequent scarring. She was prone to the eruption of blackheads and was sure she could feel them move through her veins, tiny coagulations of dirt inching up through vessels in her neck like small mites or insects curled in egg shapes, clustering in pockets of fat, enlarging and finally corrupting her face. She imagined her whole body as a blackhead and waited in her dreams for it to rupture and her life to ooze out, leaving merely an ugly stain on the floor.

Now as she looked in the mirror she found herself placing her hand underneath her mother's chin and raising it so that it reflected beside her own. Olan had her eyes closed, was completely relaxed and allowed her daughter to pressure and shift her at will. Looking at their faces together Liano's lip corrugated upwards in an involuntary grimace. Framing her mother's face with her palms she stretched the skin back until the image was momentarily mongoloid in appearance. Liano tried to suppress a laugh but couldn't. The thought of maintaining this version of her mother appealed to her. Her eyes appeared to scan the table in search of steel pins to push at angles into her cheeks. Her speculations were interrupted when it became clear that Olan was in some pain.

Liano glanced down quickly and saw Olan's fingers curl into a fist. Just as she was about to lash backwards Liano slammed her mother's forehead down onto the wooden table. There was a sharp intake of breath. Liano looked to her right, located the position of a small sheathed knife then discounted her need of it, deciding instead simply to fasten her arms tightly around Olan's upper body. Olan turned her head and spat. What Liano whispered in her ear had the insistence of an order which could not be disobeyed.

'Relax mother. Forget it happened.'

Wiping the spittle from her face she mixed it into Olan's scalp. Again she took up the ivory comb and with fluent strokes untangled lengths of hair. Olan was shaking and rubbed her forehead in an effort to ease the pain.

Some minutes later Liano leaned over, gently kissed her mother's beautiful cheek and began talking.

'I don't know if you heard me but I left early this morning. I expected to see someone. You know how it is, one day you wake up and you say to yourself, 'today's the day'. I thought I felt someone trespass on our line. I ended up walking as far as Bradaz. But there was no one there.'

Her voice trailed off.

Liano looked out the window down to the garden below. Illuminated by moonlight she could see through the massive palm leaves to a glimmering section of pond full of lily pads and crocus flowers. She could hear the wing beats of night birds, the scratchings of animals as they moved through subcurrents of leaves and gnawed into patterns of bark. She could hear things perish and imagined long-necked birds swallowing toads and snakes, of life in the garden scrambling over roots and massing in the centre like impeded sand, and then of everything speeding up, the weight and structure of life melting down, of savagings and instantaneous regenerations, of patterns altering before her eyes like a continually reorientating state of degeneracy.

Liano looked down at her mother and again had the image of her flesh as clay. Nevertheless she kissed her sensually, enveloping her ear with her mouth, pressing the tip of her tongue into the centre of wax, nibbling the lobe.

'Look what Mola uncovered near the entrance to Bradaz.'

Liano took three truffle bulbs from her dress pocket and paraded them under Olan's nose.

'I'll cook them tomorrow with some eggs. Here, you can keep one under your pillow tonight.'

Olan remained seated at the window, gazing far off, as though she was prospecting for some form of revenge, a new discipline to impose on her daughter whom she could feel getting stronger with each passing day.

Liano looked back at her before leaving the room. Olan seemed at that moment to have a composure, resilience and majesty of which Liano could only dream. A resilience which would not be diminished by anything she did. Her mother was substantially achieved and powerful, someone she imagined who could look only with scorn and pity at the thing she had produced in the way of a child. Liano could feel that scorn now as Olan moved to her bed, extinguished the light and lay under the covers. Liano remained by the door for a long while looking in. Moonlight gave an individuating aura to the room, offering everything its shadow.

Finally Liano walked down the stone stairwell to the entrance of the main vestibule. As she stood under the huge marble arch she began to speak. The words were ostensibly for her mother, not that she would ever hear them or ever want to. As Liano spoke, the sounds of animals and birds rose and fell to the rhythm of the full moon's lunar waves.

'I stand in your shadow, licking its clean lines, trying to fill its outline with my body. My deepest anxiety is that I will never stand next to you as an equal, never believe that I am all that you ever wanted me to be, never kiss you with a daughter's deep chasteness.

'I am your daughter only when you want me.

'You have always left me to my own devices, always stood aside from me, eating alone, maintaining your unities within the Fortress, wallowing in the pit of the garden. All I do now is begrudge you my body and leave you to yourself.

'Still, something could be reclaimed, mother, if for once you showered me with attention, allowed me to live with you, let me be part of your explanation of things and figure with the flowers as part of your version of an ideal arrangement. My expectations are in accordance with what I have experienced. They are minimal.

'Just once let me understand the path you have ordained for me or let me go. Let me find my own way. How could I fail you, if you trusted me? If you loved me. You are my mother, the source of my power.

'I am alone. Always waiting for you. Listening to you when you speak. Listening for myself. Appraising the difference. I am alone without you. With you, I am more alone.

'Gone are the days when I could find some comfort in you, when your touch was special. Now when you touch me all I can feel is your coldness. I am not part of the touch. What you touch is abstract. I do not understand my part in it. I do not understand your part in me.

'Our silences go before us like shadows. Our love is a masquerade, a tacit thing, while our store of language shrinks day by day. Soon it will die back to an infinitesimal seed and wait for another generation of rains to draw it forth.

'When will we go, mother? We've been here so long, you and I. The garden is fine, it's beautiful even, but there's more. I mean I want to see something else. If father were here he would take me. He wouldn't be afraid to take me south. I just want to see it once, that's all. I can't go on my own. I've tried to convince the travellers to take me but they shy away. They know who I am. You've told them. Even the children run away. They cry out. I plead with them to come back but they just huddle together in a circle and drift out of sight.

'Sometimes I fantasise what it would be like to be surrounded by people, to have someone other than you to talk to, someone to whom I could tell everything. You've never been any help to me. You don't talk to me. Father will come back and take me away. How would you like that? Sometimes I imagine him sitting in a great house in Doan with his new wife, singing to her gently, remembering me.

'Do you remember the moment that you came to despise me? When you screamed against Eighad, you screamed against me, against the evidence of his flesh in me. I am the disaster. I am the one you hurt, the one you want to be rid of. You squander no tears on me.

'It becomes harder and harder to say anything at all. We move between each other in the kitchen, saying nothing. For weeks at a time no words are exchanged. We are both dead to each other. Let us finalise things.

'I hear you tell it again. How well it all started. It was idyllic, you say. Mother and daughter. Nothing could have been finer. I was happy then too, you say. Now look at us! We wander around the garden in the same way each day. We pass each other by. We do certain chores together but we might as well not see each other. We rarely touch. When we do I experience nothing but hate, for myself, for you. We are nothing in the act but buttress and battering ram, tremblings of a considered fever, everything shared by us in this way diminishes us.

'Let us go, mother. Let us go.

'On our journey south, I will be a good listener. Everything you've tried to teach me in the past can be gone over again. We will make a formidable duo. We will walk side by side like two parts of the same seed, in step together. We will trade stories.

Mother, in our next night of ecstasy can I clamber on your back? I want to be lavishly within you when the nightmare comes. I want to plunge my hands into the centre of your bones. I want to listen to the mirrors break between your ribs and see animal spirits fume from your mouth. Later I will listen to you explain the passageways and tunnels of the Fortress as a labyrinth, entrances that go back to the source of the world. You move through them screaming different words. All of them mean Eighad.

'Mother, I stand naked in reverence to you. Naked, I ask you to hurt me. I am your daughter. I tempt you because I know you. I know there is no other. There will never be anyone else. Our hatreds achieve too rich a reward in each other for that to happen.

'I am witness, mother, to the terror you have brought on yourself. You have staked yourself out for it, commended your body to the darkness. I find you in corners slandering the night, striking at it with blades and curses. The vices of your years have spread into the tubers and roots of the garden. Your demons have entered the realm of the garden. They curl up in the fibrous tails of samask leaves, they vibrate in the grotesque cone webs of cob spiders. It is evil that shakes the baba plants and makes them stretch out and curve around me.

'Every night now the desert grows quieter while the garden ruptures, spilling out over the ruin of the Fortress, prizing us open. If you have made your choice, mother, then let me make mine. Let me leave before the garden collapses on top of us. Your gestures disturb everything. The birds are growing ugly. What have you done? All night I hear the animals copulating but what they breed are dreadful things full of deformities. The garden's beauty is degraded, its organisation compromised.

'I have shadowed you for too long, mother, now I am leaving. You have heard me say it before, but this time I will take enough supplies with me and go south with the next caravan. I will deny your parentage. I'll not haul your history on my back any longer. I don't hold that the covenant of our bond is sacred. Just because you tamper with me in the night or that I move over you with stones and polished branches doesn't mean that I am bonded to you forever.

'I walk the boundaries throwing spells. I do tricks at will but only caged animals adore me. Do you think this is all I want? You have discarded what you have grown tired of. Still you need me. When your skull is sectioned by nightmares you cry, daughter, daughter. I despise you.

'When I say that, I realise I have reached the apex of what we feel for each other.

'Sometimes I think I am nothing more to you than a source of energy, a circumference to be broached, breached and the inner elements manipulated to your design. I am not coveted as I imagine a lover is coveted. You do not speak to me with the same passion as you speak of Eighad. He remains the prize of your hatred.

'You conjure him up and hurl yourself at him, spitting your soured anger, overblown and flowing after years of containment. I've seen you talk to his imagined presence. You mock him with your body, itching for him to advance on you, shuddering when he does, spitting in his face.

'Your tussles with the spirit of Eighad are another sign of your madness. It is a dance of parts, of shadows made fluent by candles swinging by reed twine from the ceiling. You copulate with this presentation of images forwarded by your mind. You are mad, mother. Not that it matters anymore.

'The other night I heard you talk to the shadows.

'*Let no one move*, you said.

'*I am the fulfilment of each of you.*

'*Clusters of grave smiles are scratching words on glass with their teeth. I go out with my basket when the full moon threatens the mind. I gather skulls with my crooked staff.*

'*There is no horror in the dead when you can finger their eyes, tweedle their teeth and crunch their bones. I clack tibias and femurs tramping a wide circle.*

'*Around me there are differentiated kinds of death, each loosening my guilt, letting it lift off like an egg from the inner wall, letting it float in the jellied glow of a translucent white liquid.*

'*Soon the last figments of this era will be erased from memory. The past will petrify and be picked like a healing scab from my side and once again I will be fit to be swollen by life into accomplishing a great act of creation.*

'Mother sleeps on my neck. She whispers in my ear with one eye cavorting in the darkness.

'*You are mad as me*, she says.

'She believes I have found the same multiplication and creation in death. She says my desires are friable or that they are her desires.

'*We are like vines*, she says.

'The muscles in my face tighten. I am tempted to hit her.

'No,' I tell her. 'We are not the same.

'I grab her long beautiful hair and tug it slightly. It is at times like this that she is aware of my strength. Of course I do not injure her. She is my mother. She tells me she is my mother. This means nothing to me. I hit her. I do this without knowing why.

'Mother. Do you love me?

'She tempers her anger and says nothing.

'Now that I am the stronger of us I occasionally do with her as I please. I tie her to a bed and flay her skin with a whip. When it is over I rub cream into the welts on her bottom and breasts. I cradle her in my arms and allow her to nestle under my long neck. This is the one physical feature we share. I find it heartwarming whenever this common link is emphasised.

'There! Mother swings in the swinging tree, the rhobo tree. She bends her legs then stretches them, moving aloft. Her head is back, her hair flowing behind her. She is among the birds today.

'Mother and I preserve a precious balance. I am no longer in fear of her as I was as a child. I have equalled her arm and laid her head on the bludgeoning stone. But in a community of two there has to be balance. I am more than willing to let her have the upper hand once in a while. Too often, though, she takes my kindnesses as a sign of weakness and schemes a vicious advance. I have to hold her continually in check.

'At other times she simply loses me. I cannot follow her lunatic course. Her nightmare actions are an assault on another world. The terms of her conquest are simple-minded. She moves in the garden like a huge cat, a comb of bristling hairs raised along her spine. She flexes and arches in the ultra light and grooves into the bark marks prizing white lala bugs from their holes, mashing them between her palms, rubbing their innards over her face and body. She disgusts me. I ask myself whether I have brought her to this. Was she always like this? With Eighad? With me? When he was sleeping, did she pressure his eyeballs and stick his flesh with darts, or is her madness informed by the memory of what he did to her?

'In the darkest nights she sings against me. She braces her back against the wall and spits my name into the air. Does she think it fragments me? I don't allow her to glean from my attitude the sustenance she seeks. She has a compendium of filthy names ascribed to me and to Eighad. He grows out of her mouth like a tape worm rooted at the basest point of her imagination. She screams that I am his daughter, not hers. This is not as radical or as abhorrent to me as she would wish. I sit and smile my ugly smile at her. She does not understand why I have resisted her wisdom, her versions of the past. Doesn't she know that I have my own list of hatreds, my own litany of loves. I continue to seek the facts of her past wherever they are hidden. She preserves her memories like beads and prays by them at night.

'When she slides with the animals of the garden you can see them recognise a ferocious counterpart. Mother has come to an understanding with the animals. She doesn't underestimate this advantage. She has made good her escape from me too often for her not to acknowledge the garden as anything other than a friend. In certain situations she has tempted me, goaded me to follow her, standing in a volume of moonlight playing the seductress, feeling herself up, prompting me to come and defile her. In anger and frustration I tell her I will kill her when she comes out from under her protective foliage. This of course is a familiar threat. We've been through all of this before. How much of this, I ask myself, is a complex game? Could either of us answer that? All I know is that we have our positions, our accords. We know what we can do, where we can go, at least for now.'

— ~ —

In the years that followed, Olan and Liano went their separate ways. There was a clear demarcation to their worlds and neither trespassed on the other's domain.

During the spring, after the rains had come, Liano would take her flock of sheep far into the desert setting up camp north of the Fortress. Depending on the intensity of the summer she would remain in the desert for four to five months out of every year, returning occasionally to the Fortress to replenish her supplies, or in the case of the date and banana groves, to harvest the fruit. These periods in the wilderness provided Liano with the sustenance, both visual and spiritual, to survive the increasingly claustrophobic atmosphere of the garden.

Olan remained almost exclusively within the walls of Aganatz, rarely venturing beyond the braid of dunes which spanned the Fortress in a wide circle. Although still very beautiful she had become hermetic, an isolated figure whose most intense relationship seemed to be with the garden itself, which she didn't so much tend as encourage to spawn and flourish until its density was almost impenetrable. She considered Liano an alien factor and by and large kept out of her way.

Liano had become increasingly impatient and intolerant of what she saw as her mother's mental diffusion and had begun to insist on the re-establishment of some kind of order within the Fortress as a whole.

After a particularly short spring one year, the thought of returning to what was virtually a jungle atmosphere was more than Liano could bear. It was vital, she believed, to reclaim the ancient pattern of the garden. A vision of order began to occupy her head. In it she saw the old walks cleared, with neat border hedges and flowers aesthetically tiered against a background of ornamental shrubs. The tangle of undergrowth and weeds in the large orchards and vegetable sections were cleared, the forests and swamp areas cut and drained. Each area became part of a systematised unity and was formally beautiful.

Returning from the desert early that summer she found her mother in a state of hysteria. She tried to talk to her but was pushed away. The garden was in a ferment. It was hot and fetid with balls of steam rising through the great fan-shaped baobab leaves. The animals and birds were in a state of panic with piercing, elongated cries and yacks wailing ominously from the upper canopy.

Liano retired to her room. When she awoke next morning she was aware of a peculiar difference in the atmosphere. The sunlight which normally spun through her window had been cancelled by foliage. Going onto the roof, she looked down over the parapet. The changes were perverse. To her eyes it seemed as though the leaves and branches were growing visibly inch by inch, with the trellis vines and ivies creeping up the walls and over the sides of the battlements. Standing in the same position she could feel them begin to wrap around her ankles and move up along the backs of her calves. Breaking them off she stepped to higher ground. The canopy had grown to such an extent that it appeared as a solid green surface with enormous broad leaves vying with each other for the light.

The basic plan of the garden which a few days previously had still been roughly visible was now completely obliterated. The ferocious wails and cries of the animals grew louder, creating a continuous volume of sound. Running down the spiral staircase to her room, she armed herself with a machete. On opening the lower ground floor door she screamed. The rate of growth was incredible. The light was olive green, creating an eerie vault of abberated trunks and spindle limbs, flumped and tangled in a complex striving for light.

Liano suspected that the great noria wheel which distributed water to the rest of the garden was out of order and that the banks of the larger channels had begun to overflow. The ground was soggy and made walking difficult. With her machete Liano cut wide swathes of laudstems and twirling bindweed and moved slowly towards the perimeter of the pond. For a moment the garden became strangely silent as though all life was suspended or holding its collective breath.

By the time she reached the clogged noria wheel, the water was up to her knees while the pond itself was covered by outgrowths of reeds and blanket flotations of enlarged lilies.

Weaving her hands through clusters of purple dracu leaves, she caught sight of her mother. Olan lay naked on a raised bed of moss, her arms hanging limply on either side. She appeared to be dead. Standing over her was a huge blue pig, his penis between her legs. On instinct Liano charged, machete held aloft. The pig turned, evaluated the threat and continued to hump into her mother. The first blow buried itself in the back of the pig's neck. A spray of blood spewed into Liano's face. She hacked again, blindly. The squeals of the pig were horrific. It stumbled sideways then charged. Mistaking a nearby trunk for his enemy, he butted it with what vigour remained in his body. Liano hacked once more and killed it.

Kneeling beside Olan, she could see her mother's body was covered with leeches and slugs. She prized out those which were blocking her nostrils. Olan took a sharp intake of breath. Moving her arms underneath the body, she lifted her mother up and slowly began to make her way to the south end of the Fortress. By this stage there was almost no light filtering through the canopy and she picked her way forward in darkness. The yips and squawks of animals seemed to draw closer as though they were massing at her back, threatening to stop her and regain their prize. Straining under the weight of her mother, she waded through convolvulus plants trying to muscle her arms to bear up. Liano pushed on towards the outer limits of the garden, her eyes searching the camouflage of vines and creepers, her whole body adrenalated to respond to the least threat.

Closing in on the wooden door of the south turret she felt some animals scratch and bite at her legs. She screamed at them which only provoked them more. Beginning to panic, she tramped forward more quickly and fell. Immediately a group of animals descended on her. She thrashed at them with the machete, warding them off. In a half crouch she dragged her mother the last fifteen feet.

—   ~   —

Once inside Liano sensed a suspension in the rate of growth as though the sustenance for their elephantine ruptures had been removed. A silence descended within the confines of the Fortress. Liano always remembered that moment as one in which her own will became an auspicious thing. It was the moment she declared her own war, her jihad on these rubbery outgrowths of her mother's blood, the moment that, according to her memory of it, the plants began slowly to retract, the animals to pacify and retreat.

She knew now that she must make a start and begin the physical labour of hacking away the lumbering glades of greenery, encouraged to proliferate by Olan, and create a manageable unit once more.

Liano believed her mother to have played a sinister part in the corruption of the garden and it was clear to her that Olan's removal from it was crucial if she were to remedy its dishevelled nature. If Liano had had the option of sending her to a sister or cousin in a distant townland she would have done so. Lacking that alternative however, she decided after some consideration, to place her in a large room in a rarely frequented part of the Fortress.

Picking up her mother's bruised and tormented body, she carried it gently to a moveable pallet. Placing a blanket over her she began to drag the pallet through long dimly-lit corridors, moist windowless anterooms, up and down ramps, through secret passageways and recessed grottoes, until finally she came to a large room with vaulted ceilings and one small window on the north side overlooking the desert. At an elevation of two hundred feet the desert spread out before her in an extensive dun-coloured plain with the serial peaks of Utann to the west. The window itself she considered too small to concede a suicidal exit and so she did not block it or strip it with bars.

Liano left some food and water by the side of the pallet, looked at her mother briefly and moved her hand in a shadow gesture over Olan's eyes. They remained open, glazed, indifferent. Locking the door she checked the other rooms along the corridor. There was a small annex close by which was free of debris or rotting artifacts. This she decided to use as a storeroom. Liano wanted to create a situation whereby she spent as little time as possible catering to her mother's physical needs. The distance from kitchen to room was too great for her to think of accomplishing the chore of feeding her on a daily basis. She would stock the annex with preserves and water, allotting Olan weekly portions which she could ration herself.

Initially Liano had thought of simply locking Olan in the room without further curtailment. On reflection she deemed it necessary to cage her. The idea of the cage had long been in her mind and the wood already cut and assorted. After retrieving its parts she set about assembling the whole.

The main area of the cage was ten feet square with the base boards made of tamarisk and the bars of ilb. It stood on squat legs with steel casters to make its position adjustable. Each of the mainframe's four sides were hinged to the base and reinforced with crossbeams. Broken into one side was a tunnel three feet high and eight feet long. This led to a small toilet compartment with a roof slot through which the head sprouted. The toilet seat was attached to a large tube which fed out to a hole below the window. The design was such as to allow faecal matter and urine to flow out and fall free of the walls down to the desert below. Later, when Olan grew accustomed to her conditions and her bowel movements had regularised, birds and other desert creatures collected at a certain spot and waited for her waste to drop. Competition was occasionally so great that birds tried to catch the cascading material in flight. A smaller cage was also available in the event of her mother needing to be made immobile or during those occasions when it was required of Liano to wash and disinfect the main cage.

During the first weeks of her incarceration, Olan seemed oblivious to her surroundings. She sat enveloped by a surfeit of ornate cushions which Liano had brought from her room and hummed a low atonal incantation for days at a time. Physically she appeared to shrink into herself as though the arterial connection with the source of her power had perished.

Liano, although never indulgent, was in the beginning meticulous in her adherence to weekly schedules of feeding and cleaning. It was this infrequent yet consistent rhythm which gradually afforded Olan a sense of being cared for, and it was the breakdown of this basic level of attention which led to a further disabling of her body and mind. Whether Liano's increasing disregard of her needs originated from absentmindedness, laziness or cruelty Olan could not decide, but the isolation and removal from the natural arena in which she had invested so much of herself, created an atmosphere of irremedial bleakness for her.

The first aspect of Olan's care to break down was her supply of water. Olan interpreted it as a manoeuvre which hit at an ancient need of hers, the need to maintain the gleaming appeal of her skin. It was vanity; she understood that. She also understood her daughter's desire to abase her beauty and make of her a vision of physical disintegration, a disintegration which Liano could observe and relish.

Although Olan tried to maintain her standards of personal hygiene, months of delinquent care meant that her hair became matted, the pores of her skin ingrained with dirt and large areas on her forehead and neck scaled or partly desiccated. She became depressed and apathetic. When Liano did choose to visit, she trivialised Olan's grievances and demands. When Olan maintained that she posed no threat to Liano's continuing work in the garden, Liano laughed in her face.

After three months conditions within the cage had deteriorated seriously. Olan, although she continued to eat sporadically, seemed to maintain the fact of her physical existence more out of habit than anything else. She no longer crawled through the tunnel to sit on the chamber seat but defecated and urinated openly on the boards of the cage or on the sheets which Liano provided for her. The first time Liano witnessed these transgressions, she rebuked her mother asking why she insisted on making things worse for herself.

'Mother, I could have left you to die. In keeping you here I have allowed you the opportunity to recoup your strength and later to join me in the task of reclaiming the garden. If this is how you repay me then I will have to think of new measures to bring you to heel. The day is gone, mother, when you can do as you please and by the results of your interference leave me at risk. The day is gone mother when you can organise things against me.'

'I am no threat to you Liano. Release me and let us begin again. There is no reason for you to keep me here, you know that. Tell me what you want. We can settle our differences. We know each other too well and have accommodated each other for too long for you not to trust me.'

Olan's voice failed momentarily. Gripping the bars of the cage she forced herself to continue.

'You have no right to alter things. Things I have spent a lifetime begetting. This is your attempt to demean everything I am and have believed in over the years. The garden is an image, a version of myself I was never able to achieve in you. I'm sorry for that Liano, I'm sorry, but leave it alone.'

With tears streaming down her face, Olan repeated her plea for Liano not to tamper with the garden.

It was remarkable how little sympathy was elicited from Liano. The look on her face was cynical, as though the calibre of her mother's reproach distilled nothing but an increased determination to continue. She believed that her mother still considered her weak-minded. Liano was not being accorded the respect she deserved and so as a further discipline she removed all of the bedding from within the cage and replaced it with sawdust. Liano knew that not only had the garden to be reclaimed, but her mother had to be transformed also. The only way she could conceive of doing this was to abuse her will and weaken Olan's personality to the point where Liano could insinuate her own ideas. She left Olan kneeling in the wood dust of one of her great trees, foul curses dribbling from her frail mouth.

It was extraordinary to Liano how quickly the garden retreated after her mother's incarceration. Although it was still a teeming mass of tangled plants and corrupted trees it was now possible to see where she should commence in re-establishing the order and pattern on which the garden was founded. She began with the vegetable plots and fruit groves in the south and moved north. The great noria wheel situated in the centre was liberated and the irrigation channels which spread out in grid formation were cleared. She levelled vast areas with passion, confident that the realisation of her extreme alternative would ultimately reward her.

As winter set in, her job became easier. She clambered up into the taller trees and lopped off selected limbs. At times she felt her purges were too extensive and sensed the garden about to react violently to her rough handling. However it seemed to lack the heart to stop her combative hand. It suffered the indignity of her pruning but all the while a mourning sound seemed to echo in the trees and in the songs of the birds.

While clearing the old routes and pathways Liano discovered elaborate sundials, belvederes with delicate carvings in the wood panels, loving words and initials scratched into the bark of certain trees, rockeries and water fountains. All of these she cleaned, repainted and made accessible for the first time in many years. This was a happy period for Liano, the more she uncovered and recovered, the more enthusiastic she became.

Inevitably however there were sections of the garden which she could not get to or which refused to be tampered with. These she was wise enough to leave alone. Also those areas which contained the larger animals were out of bounds to her. But by and large, after six months or so, the garden had regained something of its old order. As her work neared an end Liano often went to the top room of the northern turret to achieve a fuller sense of what she had accomplished.

By spring when the bulk of her extravagant work was complete, Olan was virtually dead. She lay in the cage wizened and dry, unable or unwilling to communicate, a tiny defeated creature who might as easily or as justifiably have been buried. Liano was later to regret that she didn't take the long sheath knife which she carried everywhere with her and plunge it into her mother's heart. Instead, on the morning when she put the finishing touches to the gravel pathways and gave the uncovered gazebos a final lick of paint, she went to her mother and prepared to release her.

Unlocking the hinged sides of the cage, she lowered them to the floor, stepped in and began to brush the sawdust and nesting insects from her mother's body. In that moment of bearing witness to her mother's degenerate and decaying body, she felt a sudden shiver of guilt and sadness. Had she brought her mother to this? What had Olan done to deserve this? Liano could not answer. Steadying herself she repeated the rationale which had made her actions necessary. It was a question of survival and if they were to survive it had to be on these terms.

Her mother opened her eyes. They were retreated, watery, unable to focus. Taking her in her arms, Liano realised how much lighter she was from the time she had brought her from the garden. She was as light as she imagined a young child to be. She carried her back through the long corridors and musty rooms until they came to Olan's old room on the ground floor. Her bed was made up with freshly starched linens. Sunlight streamed in, highlighting a small table supporting a vase of large yellow blossoms.

When Liano laid her down on the bed, Olan turned her head slightly settling her eyes on the yellow flowers in the great bowl beside her. She began to cry and muttered something in Liano's ear. Although barely audible, Liano knew what it was she wanted.

'I'm sorry, mother, I can't let you touch them just yet.'

Olan rested her head back on the pillow and continued to stare at the flowers.

The long weeks leading into early spring passed and little by little Olan's strength increased. Liano felt the time was right to take her mother into the garden and to show her what she had done.

Liano placed a large olive-green rattan hat on Olan's head and wheeled her out through the outer rooms of the ground floor, settled her in brilliant sunshine and offered her a first glimpse of the garden in its new form. Liano was captivated by the tremors of shock and the look of disbelief which registered on her mother's face. Before her there stretched a wide gravel path of white stones with neat borders of delicate flowers rigorously tiered. Liano continued to stand behind her mother exuding the sense of having fulfilled a longheld ambition. Some birds flittered from shrub to shrub and held forth in full-throated song. It was obvious that Olan despised what she saw and in those first views of the garden understood why she had suffered so much. Something approaching hate glimmered in her eyes.

Olan had seen enough and demanded to be taken back to her room. Then she dismissed Liano. Liano was to chart her mother's real recovery as beginning at that moment when through some gift of power she managed to reclaim an ancient sense of herself and of the substantial inner focus which had decided her fate and her survival through the trials of her life. Liano was content with this adjustment which in a way inhibited the expansion of her own guilt. Secretly she wanted Olan to be strong again.

Some days later Liano stood by the window in her room and looked out on what she had achieved and the great effort which had been demanded of her. She realised how diminished she felt by the whole exercise. She was exhausted. It was as though she had come to the end of a physical and mental rotation and now needed a new focus to revive her energy and invigorate her spirit. She needed to get away from the garden. Her fingers reeked of decay, her head full of deranging corruptions. All she wanted to do was walk, to weigh her eyes with the colour of sand, to feel sand rather than the cloying texture of fragmenting leaves beneath her feet. In the distance she could see the scars and ridges of the great mountain range of Utann and further south the dark isolated conical of Bradaz. In a few days, she decided, she would take the sheep towards the southern perimeter of Aganatz and camp there a while.

Liano went to see Olan. In the months since her release her mother had slowly begun to reclaim her once commendable beauty. She was beginning to lose the wizened aspect acquired in the cage. The wrinkles on her face had smoothened out, her eyes had clarified, her bones were covered with flesh. She had taken to going off on her own. Sometimes Liano followed her. Rarely did she take the same route twice but her destination was always the same. Liano moved through empty rooms and looked in through the bars of a small window at the end of a white corridor.

Olan sat on the bare ground in the far left-hand corner with a huge pointed straw hat on her head, her face covered by a black veil, her shoulders by a maroon cloak with tiny knots along the braided edge. She untied these one by one, haunting the air with invocations, bleating her curses into the shadows.

'Are they against me?' thought Liano. 'Are they her words I feel roil in me?'

Suddenly Liano felt vulnerable. She swivelled on her heels sensing the approach of some force from behind. Olan fanned her indigo coloured fingers across her face. Through the slits in her veil Liano could see her focus her between the bars.

'I am available to her evil,' thought Liano. 'I must have that strength. I must rebuff this, this her first speculation of violence. Mother lures me to it. This rite. She's pulling things up through the floor, restitching shreds of flesh which have been torn from her. She is fitting herself out, designing her flesh dress, decking her body with wounds and signs, demarcating her difference, re-establishing her power.

'I love you mother,' said Liano. 'Don't go so far away from me.'

Olan knelt on all fours and tramped around the corners of the room increasing her pace until her figure blurred between the bars. Her clothes flew off like kites or bird wings reeling backwards. Her eyes protruded like plant bulbs pushing her forehead up against her hair. When she stopped, her clothes remained embedded in the wall. She stood in the far corner of the room naked, her face painted cobalt blue with hennaed stripes down her nose and cantan petals pinned around her eyes. She ran her finger along the plaster of the wall, split it and folded the sections apart. She took a deep intake of breath and pulled out a long plantain. She looked at Liano.

Liano cried, 'Mother! Mother!'

She took three enormous steps and tried to enter by the door. It was locked. She kicked it and screamed, then returned to the window. Olan had the fruit in her hand and Liano watched as she broke the flesh in two and proffered a half to her. As Liano reached through the bars to touch it the plantain became a viper seamlessly connected with her mother's arm. Olan laughed while Liano gazed on her mother's transformed body. Her muscles were firm, beautifully toned, her breasts punched out, the nipples hard and pointed.

Olan moved her body into a dance, sexing her curves, twirling her upraised arms like fluent snakes, gyrating her hips and bottom. Liano tried to resist the physical charge of her body but she could not. Olan wove around the room stopping in a side profile before the window and began to copulate with an imaginary animal, taking the sex into her groin, arching her body, gasping, her bottom muscles tightening and loosening, her tongue curling upwards towards her teeth as she screamed from the back of her throat. Liano moved her hand beneath her dress, pushed two fingers into herself, then three.

From sunrise to late evening of the following day Liano remained in the garden trying to stem the rate of growth which was threatening to overwhelm the pathways and ornamental hedgerows. It was a pointless exercise since she found that she could not match the ferocious will motivating the regressive fecundity which spawned around her. She knew that Olan was at the root of this subversion of order. The garden had once more become a remedial atmosphere for her.

Liano walked along the red and white tiles which covered the floor of the north turret and looked out on the desert. Her whole body relaxed immediately. The sun projected the Fortress in shadow far into the desert. It was a benign reflection, an antidote to the reality of the garden, a liquid rendition into which she could infuse like sugar. She felt lightened by this perspective as though a stockade of stones had fallen through a cleft in her belly.

The desert itself was flecked with gravel densities and occasional clusters of basata shrubs. Keeping her eyes focused on the small mounds and defiles, she scanned the ground for infinitesimal movements which would describe the presence of a lizard. She had a kinship with these creatures who were so secretive, so decisive. She watched them slash their tails into the sand and plod their chicken claws towards cavities scooped out from the banks.

As the sun declined Liano reflected on all that had passed. She could feel her mother mustering herself against her, stretching her fingers back into the garden, letting them grow up through the pink tresahab roots, breathing the dangers of the garden back into her system, weaving a serious violence against her. She understood now the impossibility of maintaining what she had arranged. Once again she felt as though a fertile antagonism had been ordained against her. She listened to the birds, expecting to hear a series of dissonant notes, a quarrelling of tones signalling her to beware. The garden's flux had become a solid thing. The sense of congestion, of blockage, was palpable. There was a certain pressure building at the base of things.

— ~ —

Liano left the Fortress early next morning with the crisp desert air brushing the hair from her face. She began to herd the sheep beyond the shadow of the high walls and out into the desert. For the first time in months she felt liberated. The clean heat of the sun warmed her skin and it was as though fresh blood flowed in her veins. It was such a relief finally to be removed from the oppressive exuberance of the garden. It was spring and she was happy to kick off her sandals and walk on the light down of grass beginning to cover the ground. Listening to the remote cackle of baba and caju birds she prodded the sheep, moving them south in a straggly line. Mola, although arthritic and almost blind, still followed faithfully by her side.

Each day they went a little further from the Fortress, setting up camp after sunset. On the seventh day, after having zig-zagged south south west, they approached the first outcrop of quartz which was part of the isolated rock both she and Olan called Bradaz. She decided to rest and allowed the sheep to feed on the new grass. From this distance and perspective the Fortress was almost out of sight with only the tips of the high white turrets visible.

As she stroked Mola, she thought back over the period of Olan's incarceration and questioned whether in her treatment of her mother she had not gone too far. Had she managed to enlarge the deposit of hatred which existed between them? Certain images of her mother's imprisonment returned to her — the sight of her naked and shivering, moving around the bars of the cage, defecating in small piles, picking at the sores on her skin and eating them. Liano recalled the night she had entered the room with an oil lamp and a long pole sharpened to a point. In a frenzy she had verbally maligned her mother, working herself up until she slid the wood point through the bars and began to jab Olan's flesh. She had watched her mother bleed, her hands gripping the bars, her teeth bared, her eyes seeming to memorise each morsel of pain. Liano had justified each drooling line of blood and named each wound. This was a violence seasoned by her past, by her mother's past in her. She had stopped only when Olan could deflect the stick no longer and lay limp in a pool of blood, her arms covering her head. As Liano stood in the half darkness with the pole held stiffly between her hands, her whole body shaking, she had heard a sobbing. She looked at her mother and realised she was crying. It was this disturbing memory which Liano returned to over and over. At that moment she had wanted to crawl into the cage, to solace and comfort, to cancel the badness, to disremember the history which had provoked the outburst and retrieve for both of them something approaching harmony.

Liano stood in the late afternoon sun, looking south to Bradaz. She stood for a moment in silence still thinking of her mother, then slowly went about rounding up the sheep for the night. They were a quarter of a mile to the west, feeding in a small hollow on some grass and basata leaves. As she went through her daily ritual of counting the flock she realised one was missing. This was a regular occurrence. On not seeing the animal in the immediate vicinity she had the choice of going in search of it then or waiting to see if it returned of its own accord by morning. In all likelihood it had wandered to the large outlying rocks near Bradaz. Deciding to go and look for it before sunset, she instructed Mola to stay with the rest of the flock.

As she walked Liano found herself resenting her accountability to the animals. Her frustration increased the closer she came to Bradaz. The sun was in descent and the light beginning to fail when she saw a familiar shape in the distance. Liano's eyes were keen but there was always the possibility that what she had focused on was merely a rock. She promised herself that if this was the case she would return and check again early next morning. As she drew closer the sheep's presence was confirmed. It appeared to be standing over or on top of something. It wasn't until she stood over the animal that she realised what lay beneath the beast was a man with one fist clenched firmly around the sheep's right leg, the other desperately clinging to the dugs.

Liano was both frightened and intrigued. It was evident that the man posed no physical threat. His clothes and skin were in tatters. Any exposed skin had been badly burned by the sun. A rough beard made it difficult to discern the quality of his features. His whole body was emaciated, his legs shredded and ulcerated. Liano overcame her initial revulsion and the thought of helping him surfaced as a secondary response. She wondered if he were still alive.

With one hand under the sheep's neck, the other between its back legs, she eased the animal to one side. The sheep kicked back, pummelling the man in the side. He groaned miserably and rolled over. Looking down on him with renewed interest Liano could see that his lips had split in several places and that he was having extreme difficulty swallowing. She tried to conceive of where he had come from but the only scenario which fitted was that he had been ostracised or abandoned by one of the caravans and left to die. Because of her upbringing and the admonitions Olan had drummed into her as a child, the thought of bringing him back to Aganatz was not the first solution she entertained. Their lives depended on the travellers' continuing belief in the leprous fiction which had been spun around them. It was imperative that no one infiltrate their boundaries. Such an interference would point the way to others and before long the Fortress would be over-run, with Olan and Liano cast out or killed.

Although Liano believed this implicitly, she could not deny her impulse to help the devastated creature stretched out at her feet. She began to conceive of him in the same terms as she did any injured thing she found in the desert. On one level her interest was undoubtedly piqued by the fact of his manhood, on another level she believed that the desert had offered him up to her. She had never been this close to a man before, never had the possibility of touching such exotic flesh. Her curiosity was intense. She was about to touch him when he opened his eyes. He seemed unable to focus or having focused to credit the reality of her presence. He raised his head a little but could not sustain the effort.

Liano began to consider her options. If he was going to recover or indeed survive she would have to bring him back to the Fortress. He needed water. There was some at camp, but better she thought to return to Aganatz, get a stretcher and pick up the water from camp on the return journey. If she left now she would be at the Fortress by midnight. The route was so well known to her that darkness posed no special problem. She wondered briefly what Olan's response would be. She registered her immediately as a threat. Perhaps it was only now when she had made her decision to aid the man, to keep him, that she began to feel protective, possessive.

'After all,' she thought to herself, 'I found him. He's mine.'

The last thing she wanted was for Olan to meddle in what was a unique discovery, her discovery. As she looked at the man again she was less confident that he would survive the interval of her absence, or indeed the journey. He was in such a state of physical dis-integration that his body seemed to be desiccating slowly in front of her. Before departing she saw that he held a piece of paper in his left hand and she bent to take it from him. His hold on the paper was fierce and she could not prize it from him. Liano collared the sheep with some rope and led it away, vowing silently to the man that she would return by first light.

PART II

Hadge lay in the dust unable to move as darkness gradually obscured the granular world which surrounded him. With his eyes closed he recalled the incident which had brought him to this, the verge of death.

Three months previously a letter had arrived from a friend in the town of Limbah inviting him to stay. It had been solicitous, with his friend insisting that he needed to be refreshed with a cosmopolitan perspective since the town offered no reprieve from conversations of sheep bladders and domestic trivia.

Hadge was a hundred miles north of Limbah at the time but considered it an opportunity to revive an old friendship and perhaps explore the territory of the great desert on the margins of which Limbah nestled as a final outpost.

On arrival he was warmly received and accommodated. Although conditions were primitive he was treated with great generosity and cajoled to remain longer than he had anticipated.

During the course of his stay, a dinner was held in his honour. Of the women who served the meal one in particular caught his attention. Her name was Sima, the wife of a soldier who at that time was serving in the far north. After the meal he inquired of his friend as to whether a meeting might be arranged. Caution was advised and contact with the woman discouraged. Nonetheless a rendezvous was established and three days later they met in secret. The affair provided him with the ideal excuse for extending what had already been an agreeable interlude in his travels. Hadge rented a small house which provided them with a discreet setting.

After some months of happy indulgence, Sima grew ill. A wasting disease slimmed her once bountiful body and left her ravaged by a series of illnesses. This coincided with her husband's return. Hadge was pressed by his friend to leave but he refused. A deep bond had evolved between the lovers and he was adamant that he would not leave her side. The affair was discovered by the husband and a rumour linked the disease to the stranger. A plot to kill him was uncovered.

With a small package of supplies Hadge was hustled to the perimeter of the desert. It was agreed that he would remain at a designated spot for three days and that new supplies would be brought when tensions relaxed. Those in search of him would in all likelihood head north, believing that the desert would accomplish their task should he choose any other route.

Hadge expressed his remorse for the trouble he had stirred in the town and reluctantly made for the spot described. He declined the offer of a knife.

Three days passed, then four and still there was no sign of his friend. He had been careful to ration his water supply from the start and believed he had enough left for perhaps five or six days. His friend was too conscientious a man for the delay to suggest anything other than a serious hitch. Hadge could not discount the possibility that he had been killed as his accomplice. To return to the town meant almost certain death, to remain where he was, inevitable dehydration. Even if his friend were alive, another visit would compound his guilt. Hadge made the decision to leave.

He knew that along the eastern fringe of the desert was a well-travelled caravan route which at this time of the year would be bringing spices south to Urdan. He drew a small map in the sand with Limbah on the northeastern perimeter and gauged that the route lay fifty or sixty miles further east. Apart from suffering some abdominal and limb pain, which he recognised as early signs of heat exposure, he felt in relatively good shape. By travelling from sunrise to mid morning and again at night he believed that a distance of twelve to fifteen miles per day was possible. His water consumption would go up, however, making the likely limit of his resources four days, maybe five.

At daybreak of the fifth day he took a reading from the minarets of Limbah and set forth. The desert stretched out before him in a seemingly limitless gravel plain with only the most minimal of undulations or sand hummocks. Plant life was sparse or non-existent. In an effort to maintain as direct a route as possible, Hadge settled on colour spots where no rocks or depressions allowed for alignment. Travelling by night he maintained and corrected his easterly course relative to distinctive constellations.

By noon of the sixth day the intense heat began to affect him seriously. Stomach cramps and involuntary spasms made walking difficult. Reduced secretion of saliva and the gradual engorgement of his tongue meant that swallowing was protracted and painful. With no cover to provide protection from the afternoon sun he could only stake his robe over himself and remain as still as possible. He sweated continuously, losing valuable liquids and minerals. He craved water. Images of glistening bowls of fresh water inundated his imagination. He steeled himself to image his body as robust and sated. The mental trick brought only momentary relief. What troubled him most was that he had at best three days to go before reaching the eastern limit of the desert and already he was seriously debilitated. By night the chilling temperatures of the desert induced a urinary release which was completely unexpected. What fluids he secreted in this way, he rubbed back into his hands.

By day seven he had slowed considerably. He continued to adhere to his system of rationing but his body had sweated to such an extent that the process of dehydration was well advanced. His tongue felt bloated and raw. His water supply had become brackish. When carefully tipped into his mouth, it seemed to evaporate or be absorbed by the pores of his tongue like a sponge.

Intense bouts of nausea and headaches made him stop for long periods. His stomach muscles churned over, involuntarily raking his throat in a series of dry retches.

Two regrets figured prominently during this period. The first was that he hadn't waited a day longer at the abutment of rock outside Limbah. One day longer would have defined his position and that of his friend more clearly. A day longer however and his option of heading east would have been cancelled. Perhaps what he really regretted was not having ventured into town in an attempt to secure a way through. His other regret was that he hadn't taken the knife. If it came to the point where he could go no further, the knife would have provided him with an efficient means to end his life. Normally he would have discouraged such a deed for himself or others but pain, he suspected, evolved a different rationale.

That night he lay down in a shallow depression of shale slivers and pebbles and tried to sleep. His robe provided little protection against the chilling night air. For short periods sleep suspended his anxiety about the increasing physical disability and disintegration he was experiencing. He could feel the particle life in him being eroded, each cell impacting slowly, his shrunken resources decreasing resistance. He tried to invoke memoried episodes of triumph over great pain to fortify himself with evidence of his ability to supersede the physical. But the putrid aroma of death clung to him. It was like a shadowy emanation, a stalking threat drawing his body down. When he woke his throat was completely dry. Stripped bare of all lubrication he knew that in a short time it would begin to tighten and constrict.

At daybreak on the eighth day Hadge noticed a change in the weather. The wind which up to now had been south south west veered north, covering the sky with a blanket of cloud. This in itself was a welcome relief but he could feel the wind picking up gradually and the air reeked of dust.

The desert took on a darker aspect with the wilderness of sand appearing to turn to ash. What shrubs survived in this climate had curled their leaves and projected their thorns. It was with considerable foreboding that Hadge continued to make for what he believed was a cluster of rocks on the horizon. By mid morning the wind had whisked dust particles into the air, turning the atmosphere a burnished orange. Visibility was reduced to ten yards and Hadge had long since lost sight of the rocky protrusion to the east. With the hood of his robe drawn completely over his face, he moved blindly, trusting to instinct, his body tremoring from the blasts of sand.

It seemed to him, later, that he had wandered in and out of consciousness. He could not be sure that he had continued walking, or if he had, that he had done so mindlessly. The force of the wind lashing against his skin had flayed it miserably. No scourge could have reduced him so efficiently. It was a measure of suffering, he assured himself, which would bring its own reward should he survive.

Late afternoon brought some respite, but even so he could see no more than thirty or forty yards ahead. The settlement of rock was nowhere in view and he felt hopelessly lost. Although the sky was occluded by dust he believed that a cloud cover was still in place. This would serve as a buffer to the stars and make the realignment of his position impossible. For days he had denied the reality of his position but the prospect of his death now loomed more irrevocably than any placement of stone.

For the moment it was better to walk than to remain still. It occurred to him that the relinquishment of the spirit was not such a difficult thing when pain suffused every pore and organ of the body. It would not be a dramatic end, simply a gradual decline into the final reality of the unconscious.

When the force of the wind increased he felt he could go no further. Kneeling on the earth he conceived of his own resting place and began to scoop the shifting layers of sand, creating a deepening hollow. He crept like a lizard into the structured hole and slept, all the while feeling something prod the wasted flesh of his side.

Instinct had brought him to the coincident grave of another soul, which on the morning of the ninth day, finding himself still alive, he disclosed. Reason, logic, probability, played no part in this discovery. It seemed appropriate to him in some ways that one spot should contain a multitude of men. A hallowed spot made potent by death, one that would attract others over time.

The remains of the body he uncovered appeared to be those of a man with the head separated from the torso. It was from beneath the pelvic curve that he retrieved a pouch containing a notebook and compass which he held in his hands.

With enough light remaining by which he read, Hadge examined the notebook with its crudely embossed covers. He rubbed sand from the desiccated leather and turned the small book over with a reverential piety. The frontispiece had as its central motif a four-turreted castellate structure with windowed spires and battlements. As though to balance the precise lines of the building, a loosely conceptualised tree filled the gold space to the right. The energy of these lines ranged to the side and corner of the cover in inspired strokes. On the reverse side was the image of a closed book with a fish indented over it. The border ornamentation was of four petalled flowers and circles interlinked.

Holding the book in his hands, Hadge felt like a diviner quivering over water veins. The fact of the book was portentous, its very substance solaced him. With the nervousness of someone opening the diary of a lover he thumbed over the cover of the book.

Inside was a blemished piece of folded paper, partly singed and rotted at its edges. Hadge teased out its fragile sections until it became apparent that what he had in front of him was a map of some kind. On the top left hand corner was a directional vein and just below it a clumsy drawing of a building which resembled a sectional view of the one on the cover. A broken dotted line in the shape of a semi-circle extended down the page. It was crossed at four points with the words Day One, Two, Three and Four pencilled opposite the various sections.

Hadge considered the map, surmising that the grave marked the end of Day Four, unless of course the map bore no relation to the man's last fatal journey. For the first time in days Hadge reclaimed a sliver of hope and he flicked through the book anxious to prove his reading of the map.

The bulk of the pages were blank with only the front section containing a splayed and almost illegible hand which leaned its rhythm to the right, filling the margins with oblique scratches. Hadge mulled over the complex pack of words until their transliteration was complete. The author's name, inscribed on a small panel inside, was Eighad. These were the words of Eighad:

Day One

The bitch is here somewhere. I can smell her presence like a thickening malefaction in my nostrils. Her hatred for me is secreted in every grain of sand. I should have killed her when I had the chance. Now her mustered strength sickens the very air I breathe. She has loosened the bonds of her malice and let it range like some atmospheric curse in the wind. I can almost touch the kited dimensions of her will. I sense her at my back. Olan, I cry. Show yourself.

But no. Hers is a scoundrel's revenge, a threat of shadows and insubstantial movements, malingerings of an obsessed mind that cannot effect its end.

You will never achieve me Olan. Do you hear that? I will disease you with words, make your flesh corrupt and inter you with curses and formulae.

Damn you, bitch. Damn you.

Hear these words and relinquish yourself. You are not beyond me. Not now. Not ever.

Of all the days to strike out and seek her. The wind's worse than it has been for months. I can barely see the outcrops of rock at the base of Bradaz. Has she motivated this storm? Be careful Eighad, do not credit her with too much or she will become a powerful figment. Still the thought returns. Why can't I dissemble the insistent voice telling me to go back, back to the Fortress, back to Aganatz.

It's the quality of the sickness in the air that makes me wary. These last weeks she has offered me presentments of herself, guises of the terror she commands, intimations of her power, hints that she believes she can match me, counter me. She was never my equal. It is a laughable affront that leads her now to believe she can withstand me.

There is no one to aid you, Olan. I will hunt you down, separate each organ from your body and feed your relished innards to the sand.

The night draws in and histories disengage themselves from memory. When I kill you Olan there will be an aptness to your end. It will be a rigorous and beautiful rotation of the unfathomable disgust you have conjured up in me. Words! Words! Just let me lay the knife between your legs. Every cell in my body will rejoice in the justness of the debauch I will enact on you. The earth will open and take you to its livid centre. The spirits will congratulate me for my decisiveness. By your death I'll be restored and your demented spirits will retreat with you.

O to be rid of this nightmare, to live aside from the constancy of your corruption. My pure strength will glow when you are nothing more than the faintest of pollutions in the soil. I live for the expected richness of that time.

The wind's getting worse. Best make for the great rock of Bradaz and shelter there until morning.

Day Two

I lay bones in spirals. Rituals which relieve the threats I feel are manifest. My strength is strangely retreated. I am bound to words. I avail of them. Why do I conceive of them as the sole relics of my power. I cannot see through this storm. Be calm.

I cannot move beyond the rock. The desert appears suspended in the sky, whole ridges of sand lofted up charging the air with dust. There are weird configurations presented in the distance, remote blotches, spindle forms wavering in the convex view. I feel this boulder is sluicing up ghoulish appearances for me. I'm reduced to rubbing amulets in an effort to alter things. I attribute this malicious season to her. This is Olan's witching mastery being brought to bear, raising the features of this landscape against me.

I was never of this place, conditioned to it yes, but never part of it. Let me be rid of it now. When I think of her, I think of the garden, her precious circumference, her outlandish quad of jungle breeding palm bulbs and frankincense trees, oils and bark to burn in the numbered cups of her pattern. The garden has its own fierce geometry, as complex and sinister as anything contained within the structure of the Fortress itself, a necromancy of forms plunged in the soil, an intimate malevolence linked to her blood. I can hear her now spelling my difference to the wind, extolling her powers and rhyming my hatreds in an intricate spell. She has laid the burden of her curse in the wind, in these fluted designs and devilments aberrating wildly. I scream against her to combat the terror. I was never of this place.

A day beneath the rock and the wind has not subsided. Apparitions glow and fade. A world of insects bind to me, making me heavy, describing to themselves the sufficient layers of my system. Each thing they say can partake of me. I can sense a disintegration in this chaos, things making snatches, hungering after moults of skin, peeling towards the blood, nibbling hairs, emitting tiny screams when their pincers rag into my veins.

What is it that makes me believe that there are strict boundaries to this atmospheric hell? If I move in a particular pattern and in one direction for long enough will I suddenly come to the sheer end of the storm? I visualise it as being contained by points which demarcate a square and that the secret is to calculate a course which will lead me to the border of this congested zone. Beyond it the sky will be clear, the desert sand undisturbed. Once deciphered the construct will collapse and at its centre will stand Olan.

Day Three

I move beyond the cave of Bradaz out into the sleeting particles of sand, which lash my body like a whip and tear into the flesh. I feel exhausted and without the substantial resources necessary to locate a kink in the storm. I should have reckoned on this and meditated more fiercely on some method of controverting her will. I'm being forced back along the northern ridge. I feel as though she is reeling in the thread, pacing in the high turret of the west wing looking out over the horizon, pricking her flesh with needles, seizing her blood in vials, making sure her suffering is commensurate with mine. Can I make no braver effort to break free of this zone and walk beyond the parameters of her power, to locate a pulse and rhythm aside from this strategy of wind?

I kneel on a swirling bed of sand and begin to collect stones of every size, encouraged by the idea that I will make a sanctuary of my own, a pile of pebbles stacked one atop the other until the first of many squares is formed, creating the foundation for a reflective and equalising symbol. I can see no longer. The wind has ravaged my eyes. The form of my sanctuary is in the shape which cordons me.

'Olan!' I call. But more in supplication than in anger. 'How strong you've become.' Reminding me of how it was once. But think of it, Eighad. What kind of union was it? It was monstrous. From the beginning it was only a question of the level of hate we would finally promote, the resentment we would endure until it corrupted us. The only energy between us was murderous, cursed. You too, Olan, will be better off without me, without the insidious weakness which has kept me for so many fruitless years locked in combat with you, never offering you what you craved most.

I loved you. We loved each other but it's difficult to distil those memories from the embittered years which have swollen up around us. It's hard to believe that there were days when we trusted one another, days when we kissed with a blessed firmness, days when the effort to stretch and touch was not reproached. I'm appalled that even now I don't understand how it all disintegrated.

Day Four

I stand marooned in this wasteland. I can no longer see the ridge which lay to the north two days ago. Where am I? I crawl along at intervals but there is no protection. I draw my robe over my head and shuffle along like a belaboured insect. The best I can hope for is a gully, a depression of earth into which I can flatten my bones and breathe until the dust again settles on this plain.

— ~ —

Hadge closed the book and looked blankly into the far distance to the south. In the temporary stillness he thought he could see the great rock Eighad had called Bradaz, like a specious dot on the horizon. He felt plaintive and deeply connected to the link of words which appealed to him over time. Eighad's words succoured him. Here after all was a man whose situation mirrored his own.

Looking at the map Hadge gauged the rock to be a day's travel and the Fortress beyond it perhaps another day. Two days. It was something to make for and better, he thought, to be in the midst of a struggle than to concede. He read over Eighad's words again and felt strange. They made him feel as though he was entering a proscribed arena, a landscape tapestried with curses, a shunned place he should avoid. Still, if there was a Fortress south of the rock and if he could reach it, then perhaps he would survive. He thought briefly of the woman, Olan, and of the relationship which had existed between her and Eighad. A mental picture of both came to mind. He allowed it to fall away knowing there were more urgent things to consider.

Hadge moved back to the grave where the feeble stack of bones seemed to describe the sand with a calligraphic clarity. The sun had risen. The liberated head appeared to sing and its note echo in quietude.

A heat haze miraged the perspective. There was not a breath of wind, nothing to diffuse the consistent belt of heat which beamed down. This was the alternate mood of the desert, as unbridled and malicious as the wind, a regnant power now swollen to insufferable proportions.

Looking down at Eighad's remains Hadge felt that his reading of the book was somehow prurient, as though he had taken part in an act of defilement, as though he had given flesh and blood to bones, had recalled the dead damned spirit of Eighad to the wastes where he would now roam without repose.

Around him the desert extended without elevation with only a few scrub bushes giving perspective to the calamity of sand. His mouth was parched, his tongue bloated and roughly coated in a fungal growth. He decided to remain within the boundaries of the grave until evening, then make for Bradaz.

When the light paled, Hadge moved reluctantly out of his hole. He felt calmer, relieved and empowered by this sequence of extra-ordinary discoveries. He had slept a little and the coolness of the desert air was refreshing. Above him some eagles whirled, settling him in their ken before moving off to the high mountains in the north.

Birds of the sun, he thought, representatives of God, ascribing to him perhaps the gift of a belated shamanic vocation.

Taking the book from the floor of the grave, he placed it with the map and compass into the small pocket of his robe. In the diminishing light Hadge again described to himself the journey he had before him. It was vital to try to reach the rock by morning. Kneeling in the spacial calm of the square, he conceived of it as a purified section embedded in chaos. What lay before him was the terror of disunities. Moonlight dripped onto night acres and he saw the lightning movements of insects, heard their cries drawling like curses, opening the silence with tongue clicks and wing beats. Hadge remained steadfastly within the grave looking for a last time on the skull now illuminated by a nourishment of moonlight, which gave it a semblance of anima-tion, an altered presence hinting at life.

Raising the skull with his hands he moved his lips to the high forehead which he kissed with all the dried chapped fervour he could muster. A movement of clouds obscured the moon and he laid the skull down in darkness brushing a few handfuls of sand slowly over the bones. Stepping out of the charmed square he walked a few yards, then looked back. Sticking up some way beyond the body was the rib like a holy sword spelling out its challenge. The bone seemed to beckon to him. Reared up like a talisman or symbol of the providential, it seemed to demand to be taken. Hadge returned and placed the curved standard beneath his robe, beside his heart.

With the compass in his right hand he followed the course of the map, wrapping his arms around himself as the desert became rapidly colder. He tried to increase his pace but his legs broke and he fell suddenly on his left side. His flesh bruised so easily now that he could not afford to be weakened further by such falls. Feeling his body grow stiff he pumped his fists trying to increase the circulation. Dispirited by his lack of energy he tried to relax and alleviate the panic and the nightmarish reality of his situation. He could feel his robe brush the sores on his back as he moved onto his right side and sat up.

In the silence he saw his life as a random vibration which in death would be absorbed by the elements as efficiently as that of any other creature. A vision came to him of his body covered by a nest of beetles: the more he pushed them off the more layers spawned over him; a seething blanket rummaging under the folds of his garment, moving over his head and face, trying to invade his mouth, rotating feelers in his nostrils, prizing open his eyes, picking his body clean, the bones subsumed by sand.

He rose, took a reading from the compass and moved south east. In over three hours he had covered little more than two miles. Without renewal of his strength he would not make the rock before daybreak.

As the night wore on Hadge struggled with his robe trying to gain as much protection from the cold as he could. His movements had become wayward, delirious, and he wondered at times whether he had not turned around and retraced his steps. When the clouds drifted from the moon he took a new reading and moved forward. Suddenly he heard the sound of fantastic wings beating a course towards him, swooping down to bloody him on talons and snatch him away. As he ran, the clamour of stampeding animals grew louder until the earth vibrated. He smelt churned dust in his nostrils. He cowered in the sand, his head bandaged by his arms. Then it vanished. He lay festooned in spirals of scrub, his face veined by giblet runs of blood.

He picked his way through rocks and debris stopping occasionally to suck on pebbles and so salivate his mouth. This did something to alleviate his thirst but more importantly distracted his attention momentarily from the pain of his struggle and the belief that he had reached the limit of his endurance. Now and then when he looked south he thought he could see the great rock as a perceptible distortion in the darkness.

Some hundred yards on, Hadge came to a scooped out disc no more than ten feet in diameter and a few feet deep. As he skirted the rim peering in towards the centre, he stopped, and looked more intently. An elongated shape stirred in the darkness. After a moment he recognised it as a lizard. He was surprised to find the reptile beyond the sanctuary of its hole at such an hour. He leaned over expecting the creature to flee but it merely changed position. Suspecting it to be injured he moved closer. The lizard began to move with the frenetic impulse of a harassed cripple, scuttling and lurching as though under a great burden. As Hadge gained on it, he noticed that one of its hind legs and part of its tail were seriously damaged. The leg was almost completely severed and trailed limply. Hadge envisioned the blood he could retrieve and spanned his fingers in search of a rock. One came quickly to hand and he pressed forward on his hands and knees.

He stalked the reptile, motivated by the idea that here was something other than himself which was weaker and more liable to perish. He sensed that its sacrifice would signal a victory of sorts, a tilting of some primal point of balance. It would be a ritual act which might instill a predatory zeal, a strengthening of his ferocious will to continue. He had no thought of eating it, simply of stopping a life and emboldening himself by the deed.

The lizard was restored in his mind's eye, all limbs connected and the struggle a lustral one. If he could kill it then victory was his, and the victory itself would become the seed for an imaginative fabrication. Forcing the issue he would enliven himself by the idea that he had not recognised the depth of his resources. The struggle would be the key to disclose a commanding physical aspect in himself.

The lizard moved away to the farthest point on the slope. Hadge hunkered down and with stealth and conviction layered himself as a threatening and inviolable shadow over the reptile. Although it made a final lunge to evade its fate he blocked its path and squashed its head beneath the rock.

As he turned the lizard over on its back, the cream-grey belly bulged like a voluptuous breast waiting to be milked. Hadge was now motivated by a level of instinctive behaviour which insisted that the quarry be eaten. Taking Eighad's rib from inside his robe he ripped the belly open and folded back the flaps of soft flesh.

The innards and blood were warm and his eyes invested them with a succulence which made him stuff his mouth full of intestinal secrets. Strings and extensions of gut caught in his teeth and trailed down his chin. He gorged muscle and skin, making sure not a trickle of blood was lost. By the time he was finished, little remained other than the bones and hard scales. He was about to throw the carcass away when he noticed one of the lizard's eyes still intact. Applying pressure to the eyeball he squeezed, levering it like a peanut into his mouth. With his belly full and the moon dispensing sufficient light by which to read, he consulted the map and compass and plodded over the hollow towards the rock.

Feeling renewed, Hadge made good progress. The sky had lightened. Dawn he gauged to be no more than two hours off. Before him lay a swarm of gravel dunes, beyond them the distinct outline of the rock rising to a spire of about six hundred feet. Excited by this, his first real glimpse of Bradaz, Hadge hurried over a surface layer of gypsum, then felt his stomach churn. His whole gut ached, suddenly disfiguring his face. His stomach heaved and he lay down winded by the pain.

Sitting hunched over, he lowered his head to his knee and stroked his belly. It felt as though parts of the ingested reptile were reforming themselves, parts locating parts until the thing lived. He opened his mouth with some sense of his freeing a caged bird, which nervously fluttered and clawed at the root of his umbilical link. He thought that what would in fact emerge would more resemble some spineless glob of flesh waddling back across the desert to its bones. The struggling, gnawing sensation became unbearable. Opening his mouth wide he retched into a hole of shifted sand. It was some time before the various half-digested parts of the animal lay before him. He covered the vomit and lay back exhausted.

Admonishing himself, he knew now that he should have let the lizard be, to wither and die according to its own rhythm. He felt dispirited, apathetic, betrayed by his instincts, blithely aware that were the instrument to kill himself at his right hand he would use it.

A light wind rose from the south and he scrambled onwards, sometimes on all fours, towards a destination which, if reached, would finally allow him some respite. Devastated by pains and sores which enfeebled his legs and arms, he began to drift in and out of consciousness. Whatever mental tension or balance had existed up to now became frayed and his mind began to wrap to the rhythm of the unreal.

He heard the voice of an old lover encourage him to move faster. 'It's no distance at all,' she said. 'You'll be there soon. I've prepared a full table for you and afterwards we'll walk in the shade of palms.'

'Liax,' he called. 'Will there be water to drink?'

'In the garden,' she answered, 'everything is made of water. The granite slabs of the perimeter are pools of rosewater flavoured with almond. There is nothing in the garden which does not liquify, even the food has an ambrosial solvency.'

'Liax,' he called again. 'How far is it to the garden?'

But there was no reply.

Hadge came to a large bed of stones some of which were lit by a delicate glow from beneath. He picked one up and saw a tangerine floating in syrup. He bent to remove it and could have sworn his fingers touched it, when it vanished. On branches of scrub he saw pears and cactus fruit oozing their sugared juice. In wind depressions sky blue water stood clear as glass. Pebbles appeared as crimson pomegranate seeds, the sand itself as a sea of milk.

The desert was bathed in the early light of morning when Hadge looked around, aware of a new placement of rock and sand. His hands and knees were bloodied and he felt drowsy and befuddled from the lack of sleep. No more than two hundred yards ahead lay the great rock Eighad had described, isolated in a wasteland of desert. Hadge distrusted the vision and turned away. The night had riddled him with horrors and illusions, and this he believed to be no more substantial than the rest. He turned to look again.

The spired rock was placed southward on an elevated ridge. The base was wide, with incursions and erosions appearing like minor defiles leading up to grooved and fluted surfaces which gave way to a broad open cone peak. The rock had a lacquered black sheen which made its isolated presence seem all the more startling. It seemed to exude an animated quality as though its centre were livid, its core laval and simmering.

Hadge continued to stare at this nobbled inverted cone waiting for it to diminish or be absorbed in air. The image remained and Hadge got to his feet. He walked forward, constructing his steps with care. The sun had now risen and light began to refract from the desert floor. Leading up to the base of the rock was a maze of closely spaced, steep-sided ravines, separated by sharp crested ridges and spurs. Encrustations and thick deposits of salts filled the abraded pockets of stone.

As he drew close to the rock he tried to recollect the words of Eighad written when he had lain under the belly of Bradaz but his mind was vapourish, decelerated, unable to net the whirling details from memory. Hadge had the sense of himself as an initiate entering a territory of power with the earth tremoring as he trespassed towards an opening on the eastern face.

It was late morning when he finally reached the umbrella of shadow projected by the rock. He felt enervated and light-headed when he looked back on the sterile plain he had crossed.

In the cool entrance of the cave he lifted his robe and examined the oozing sores and abrasions on his legs. There was a leprous quality to the lesions. Gently he drew the robe down to his ankles, placed his cheek against stone and tried to sleep.

But the darkness at his back seemed to conjure a bestial presence. A malaise of spirits was waiting for him to lapse into sleep. When he did they would uncoil from breeches in the earth, tower over him and draw him into their world. He was unable to temper his head or level the evil he imagined permeating the rockface.

Was it not time, he thought, to concede, to roll his body up and lean into the rumouring rock, to decline further effort and advance an end?

From a distance Hadge's body was barely distinguishable from rock, blood being the roseate difference. It was now ten days since he had left his place of hiding on the outskirts of Limbah. Easing himself up slowly from within the cave he looked out over the expanse of sand, feeling the granular world beneath him seethe and infiltrate his pores. On the horizon, dust wavered like wax flames arcuated to spend their power in a violent pattern.

Occasionally when he laid his ear into the wind he thought he heard the sound of a bell holding and reverberating.

Deadening his nerves he created a carapace of his body, a retreated energy already buried. He could sense the erosion of his spirit, the memory of his resilience now appearing as a ridiculous affront, a foolish burden endured through hope.

He felt betrayed by time, by an absurd pattern which refused to deliver him up. At times he conceived of the desert itself as a phantom — like the host of illusions which had badgered him, it too would finally evaporate. His stubbornness in the face of pain was due in part, he felt, to the fact that he had never considered this style of death for himself. It was not a death he had ever approached. He could feel the material of his robe melded by oozes of pus and blood to clusters of sores. His legs looked like brittle twigs blackened by bruisings and clottings.

As morning wore on Hadge crept to the mouth of the cave. Once again he thought he heard the pang and echo of a bell sound in the silence. Ahead of him lay the great horizontal plain leading to Aganatz.

Panning the surface he settled on a dark object perhaps quarter of a mile away. He had no reason to suspect it as being anything other than a visual illusion. Still there was something different in its aspect, in the way it moved, in the manner in which it persisted. Whatever it was, it walked an irregular pattern, zig zagging across the desert, stopping for incidental periods of time. In the course of the hours that followed Hadge thought it to be a man, at other times a dog which had perhaps wandered from one of the caravans. It was mid afternoon before the shape was finally clarified. It was a sheep. A black sheep with a copper bell hanging from its neck. It had begun to wander towards the rock and was now no more than a hundred yards beyond the mouth of the cave.

Hadge crawled slowly down the steep ridge leading to the desert floor. If he could tether it, he thought, then whatever milk remained in its dugs might revive him sufficiently to complete the last leg of his journey. Tearing a strip of cloth from his robe he twisted and knotted it. The sheep, although by now aware of him, did not appear ill at ease.

Hadge slithered towards it on his belly, wishing he could make some clicking sounds with his tongue to placate the animal. Once he was within a couple of feet, the sheep moved towards him and smelt his hair. Gently Hadge placed the noose around its foreleg and eased himself underneath its dugs. The sheep was rank and Hadge suspected a hidden wound, something which had soured in the heat. Taking one of the teats he nervously pulsed the membrane with his fingers. The sheep jiggled from side to side and a few drops of liquid fell on his skin. Manoeuvring again he drew another nipple into his mouth and sucked until the initial spits of liquid began to fill his throat. Hadge felt an immediate scintillation of his system, every molecule was sensitised, identified. In that moment he visualised his body's return to normality.

When Hadge awoke it was dusk. Standing over him was a figure dressed in a red robe. It was a woman with her face partly hidden by a veil. Feeling himself condemned to visions which insinuated themselves like delicacies into his consciousness, he looked away. The image remained and he examined it more closely.

She appeared to be young although it was hard to tell. He tried to say something to her but his voice failed him. He gestured but she took no notice. She in her turn seemed to be scrutinizing him. It was as though she was calmly evaluating whether it wouldn't be best to leave him, after all he seemed barely alive.

Although her eyes were shadowed by the veil he sensed an imperious gaze and an egret-like trace in the angled line of her neck. Inevitably she was curious, why else would she remain looking at him for so long? With his robe lifted to his thighs his damaged legs must have been a difficult sight to stomach. He had no idea what his face looked like, undoubtedly grizzled by the sun, a beard masking his once amiable features. It was obvious that he posed no physical threat so she could afford to be syllogistic in determining what course of action to take.

The woman remained in the same position for so long that Hadge conceived of her as being iced to the point of immobility. Visualising it from above, they could all have been dead, a trinity of forms stiffening in the last light of day. Unable to appeal to her, he wished finally that she would go away. Shortly after that she bent down, tied a short string around the collar of the sheep and led it away.

Hadge was glad she was gone, sorry that she had taken the only physical comfort he had left. As night descended he shivered once more in the cool desert air. When the moon rose it was voluminous and starch-white. Hadge looked at it, feeding his eyes into its centre. The longer he looked the more insistent became the waves of light emanating from it, until he felt assuaged by them, and the moon became the visual reflection of his spirit.

He folded his arms around his chest and began to rock to and fro, the night air moving like steel points through to the margins of bone.

It had been such a long time, he thought, since he had known the comfort of a fire or let his head fall onto a pleat of cloth worn by someone he loved.

But there was no one waiting for him. No one, knowing he was dead who would not carry on with but the most perfunctory of farewells. What did he expect? He had not after all thrived in one community for long enough to be known as anything other than an ideologue, a wanderer, someone whose intimate range was never broad enough to contain another for very long. He was too brittle, too detached in the context of love, too remote. To this extent he was imbued with a sense of failure, the failure to abide, to be steadfast, resolute in something other than the conviction that to move on was as much an imperative as breath to his continuance.

He had never stood with the bountiful gatherers reciting their vision, or waited for them to press their prayers like knives into his ears. They told him that sooner or later he would be restrained, marked with the symbol of the outcast and hunted down by a crowd of townspeople. According to their sense of justice they would make of him a misshapen alternative.

Disturbed in the course of the night by insects which moved over him Hadge turned and tried to brush them off. He was withered, bereft of the enviable strength to rise and walk away from them. He was beyond weariness and waited in a state of repose for the moment his heart would relinquish its hold. He waited for death, conceived of now as a reward, a consolation, a gift he would unwrap and celebrate, a status which would allow his extinguishing body, vouched for by the dust, to finally wither and corrupt.

PART III

Liano left Mola with the flock and pressed on quickly towards Aganatz, making an inventory as she went of the things she would need in her attempt to save the man. The night was calm though starless and as she neared the great entrance gates she hoped she would not confront her mother. Over the course of her journey she decided to settle the stranger in Eighad's old room and she went there first to clear it out and prepare the bed.

In the years since Liano's first discovery of the room, little had changed. Although she had continued to go there frequently throughout her childhood she had allowed things to remain much as she had found them. Layers of dust now stood as an indication of her reverential indolence. All of this had to change. Opening the large window facing out onto the garden she allowed the brisk night air to sweep through. Taking a coarsely bound broom of twigs she gathered together a huge pile of debris — hair, decayed insects and matted fibres. The speed and energy with which she managed these tasks were remarkable. Books, pigments, brushes, papers, pens, all were placed in a large trunk, while the few articles of furniture which remained were pushed into one corner. The large bed which dominated the far end of the circular room was moved to one side and the floor meticulously scrubbed and dried.

Fresh linens for the bed were brought from a large closet in the west wing and the woven rug taken to the courtyard below and beaten. Her labours complete, Liano stood by the lintel of the doorway and surveyed the room which by the light of the oil lamps appeared pristine and glistening.

The stretcher she retrieved from the main storeroom. Buried under wood remnants and tools she dragged it out and examined it. The base was made of a single piece of board which, as she ran her hand over it, she could feel was badly splintered. She made a mental note to bring a small rug with which to cover it. The thick netting strung through a series of holes in the baseboard was largely intact. Liano then went to her bedroom to get some pillows to cushion the stranger on the route home. Liano felt exhilarated and excited. She went briefly to the kitchen to get an extra canteen of water before setting out on the return journey to Bradaz.

Liano struck out with the net pallet slung over her shoulder. In the kettle-black light of early morning her anxiety forwarded a series of grim possibilities.

What if he's dead, or dies on route?

What if Olan tries to kill him?

She harboured doubts about her ability not only to rescue the man but to restore him to health. Looking skyward she believed she saw the wheeling configuration of carrion over Bradaz. Her pace quickened as she imagined his flesh being shredded, his organs pecked to ribbons. She would reach the spot, she told herself, and there would be nothing left for her but a carcass of white bones. It was only now, with this human gift within her grasp, that she realised how desperately she wanted something to call her own, someone other than Olan with whom she could develop a friendship. Up until now she had never conceded this as a possibility. Now there was the man. It was more than she had ever hoped for. Once again she quickened her pace until she was almost running. The sky had lightened and Bradaz reared up about half a mile in the distance. Against her will, the words Olan repeated to her as a child rang in her ears —Those who trespass on our ground are outcasts, murderers, menials, madmen. Of all those who exist beyond the borders of Aganatz, they are the most dangerous. Do not touch them. Do not let them touch you. Remember, Liano, we are enough for each other. There is no reason to be tempted.

Now it was time to follow her own instincts. But her strength of purpose suddenly failed her as old fears and inhibitions forced their way to the surface. She might have been tempted to turn back had not the forcible image of the wounded man appeared to her.

Surely, she told herself, this man is incapable of committing a violence against us. This man, she confided to herself, is a sign of hope, a divine interference who will alter things for the good. As she walked on she gave more credence to this expectation. He had been sent to her, to alter the nature of her dependencies and break the seal of her bond with Olan. She had a vision of him standing in the centre of the garden with an iridescent glow surrounding his body, while Olan like some derelict in the background was sucked away, eventually filtering through a small hole in the north wall and vanishing forever. It was a vision of a new order, an indivisible unity.

The sky had fully lightened when Liano finally reached the first of the great boulders around the circular fringe of Bradaz. When she saw the intact shape of the man her heart rose. Hunched over by the burden of the pallet, she ran awkwardly like a harassed cripple. She was out of breath when she reached him. Leaving the pallet to one side, she looked down on him compassionately. He was crumpled up, his damaged hands fisted into tight knots. He didn't appear to have moved at all and she wondered if he were dead. Bending down she touched his shoulder and turned him over. His eyes were open and he looked at her with undisguised terror. Whatever he had expected to see or whatever he believed he saw had the effect of disfiguring his face. To break the spell of his fear Liano spoke to him firmly.

'I am Liano,' she said.

The words hung in the air like glass.

Drawing the pallet up to his side she whispered.

'I have come to take you home.'

It was impossible to know whether he heard or not, but he seemed to relax and closed his eyes. Liano laid out the pallet parallel to his body, folding back the flaps of netting so that she could slide him onto the covered baseboard. When she went to touch him she felt awkward

and shy, as though she was some lumbering giant who by the brutish-
ness of her manipulations might snap a bone or lift whole layers of
muscle tissue from his body. She treated him as she would a fragile
thing, like a casing of snake skin about to flake and crumble to dust.
Working her palms gently underneath his body she shunted him over
bit by bit until finally he lay compacted on all sides by pillows.

Taking a small segment of white cloth, she soused it with water
and spread it over his face. She repeated this a number of times, then
raised her left hand. Initially she dribbled only a small quantity over
his seared and blistered tongue, gradually increasing the amount.
Before moving off Liano spread a thick transparent grease over his
mouth, nose and forehead. He was insensible to all of these ministra-
tions. As she tied the straps over his body, the sun rose steadily in the
east.

After putting in place a hood of dense black cloth, she moved off.
She could feel a tremendous tension in her shoulder and thigh
muscles as she tried to keep the pallet steady and flowing at an even
pace. She felt in control and profoundly directed both mentally and
physically. There was a clear end to this effort and the desperateness
of the situation made her push herself to an almost vulgar physical
extreme.

During the course of the journey Hadge lay in a stupor, his body
virtually immobile. His face communicated the sense of his having
passed a threshold of suffering.

The sound of the pallet scraping over the desert floor reverberated
in the silence, attracting the curiosity of animals; mostly lizards and
moles who sprang to the crest of their mounds or stood startled under
the low branches of ashab shrubs. The sun was directly above them
as Liano mounted the final ridge and began the slight descent to
Aganatz. She stopped here for a moment to recoup her energy and to
check that the man was alright. Dousing her robe with water she once
more moistened his face and mouth. The water stung his face and,
jerking his head, he opened his eyes.

Hadge stared intently for a few moments at the building ahead of him. It appeared to have four white towers or minarets with the heads of elegant palms shooting up above the indented battlements. The main part of the building didn't appear fixed. Sections seemed to merge and subtract themselves so that individual strata slotted in and out of position giving the whole structure a lopsided appeal creating an impression of architectural flux. In an effort to focus this rickety vision he peered at one point on the parapet. He thought he saw the outline of a figure but could not be certain. Liano pressed gently on his shoulders and he lay back.

Liano took up the slack and marched forward towards the gates of Aganatz. She was preoccupied with thoughts of her mother and prepared herself for the worst of eventualities. Once within a hundred yards of the walls she felt a new level of physical acuity charge her body. If there was going to be a confrontation she was ready.

Olan, meanwhile, stood in the nook of the southern parapet watching Liano draw closer. She had tabulated her movements throughout the night, had watched her retrieve the net and renovate Eighad's old room. It was impossible for her to figure her daughter's intentions but she suspected a new range of aggressions were about to be perpetrated against her. Perhaps Liano had it in mind to imprison her among the hideous remnants and artifacts of the man she hated. She would fight to the death against such a ventilation of violence.

As Olan continued to look out over the desert she felt remote, as though she was watching a sequence of events which were familiar, which taken together signified something she could name or understand. These actions had a deeper range and mirrored or paralleled a pattern in her own past. It was a movement of events she felt she had to intercept. If she was sure of one thing it was that these actions posed a threat, and to allow the pattern to fulfil itself was as good as asking death to labour over her. On a subliminal level she could feel a system of energies finger in the holes and ruptures of the Fortress as surely as if someone was parting her legs and striking into her body.

In preparation for Liano's return Olan had gone to her room and dressed in her most flamboyant clothes. She clipped collars of silver around her neck, and to her ankles tied bracelets of turquoise. A headdress of fern-green silk fringed with pendant baubles fell to her shoulders. Her robe was deep blue, her face black with yellow bands streaking her cheeks. From her wrists hung tiny bells and tassels, and when she moved the clatter of her armour made the whole garden tingle in anticipation. She looked like some alternative creature drawn up from the depths. She moved like an animal closing in on its prey.

Olan continued to watch as Liano struggled with the weight of her burden. Liano's actions were considered. Whatever lay on the pallet was something she valued. Olan had seen her manage injured sheep before but never with such care. Liano was less than two hundred yards from the gate when Olan finally discerned the shape of a body cradled amongst some rugs and pillows. What she had secretly suspected was confirmed. Taking a curved sword from its sheath she descended the stone steps at the north east end of the battlements and hid in the dense shrubbery to the left of the gate. She tried to whisper a warning to Liano.

'Leave it back where you found it. It can have no place here.'

Suddenly an image of Eighad lifted off from the side wall of her imagination, like a dark bug in a deep casket unexpectedly released. Doesn't my daughter believe me when I tell her one such as this will irritate her whole world? Maybe she has understood and is returning him here so that I can enjoy the spectacle of his end.

Perhaps she has not the guts to kill him and will ask me to accomplish the deed. Silently she will move off to the far end of the garden. Later she will ask me questions.

Did he say anything before he died?

Did he cry out?

I'll tell her that I gave him every opportunity to disclose the reason for his trespass. When he continued to lie, I killed him.

I'll tell her that my action was fluent.

His head did not even roll from the pallet board.

As she waited, Olan's anxiety began to find its reflection in the garden. Blue silambaze petals fell like winter leaves. Lime trees shivered as a brisk wind whipped through the upper branches. Olan gripped the handle of the sword and waited for the door to open. She stiffened when the right half was pushed in slightly.

Liano, entering first on her own, checked to make sure Olan was nowhere in sight. The wind was now so strong within the walls of the Fortress that the great blago trees were beginning to bend. Liano screamed out at her mother.

'Wherever you are mother keep away from me. He's mine. I'll kill you if you come near me.'

Liano dragged the pallet through the partly opened door, then locked it. The entrance to the north turret was at the end of a pathway which ran between the edge of the garden and the inner wall. Liano pulled the pallet, walking backwards so as to protect the man from attack.

Olan moved through the dense undergrowth, her ankle bells ringing and mingling with the wind. She could smell his rottenness, a foulness rooted in her nostrils, and she knew she had to cut him down.

I will have to kill them both, she thought.

As she moved parallel to Liano, flowers began to wither on their stems and acrid juices ooze from porous barks. She imagined slicing their bodies up quickly, burning them, taking their charred remains to a wild part of the garden and burying them in a vacated animal dwelling. She imagined herself alone.

She thought, the plants are my companions, my truest mirror.

Kneeling down, Olan examined her quarry as he was dragged along. She could see that Liano was exhausted. The veins in her legs throbbed and the ropes had seared the flesh on her shoulders. She was on the point of collapse.

Liano, listen to me. I will cater to your every need, only let me kill him.

But no, she is at the age where she believes she must establish her own rhythm. She insists on doing things her way and pushes me to one side. Of course in my wisdom I understand her frustration. She needs a different kind of dominion, a different form of relinquishment. She threatens me because she does not understand the nature of her own desires.

She says, keep off. This one is mine.

I cannot imagine what has provoked her to save such a specimen. He appears dead. Even if she manages to revive him he will be good for nothing. He will distort things between us. He will consume our food. He will demand to be catered to. Slowly he will find his strength and begin to lord it over us. Perhaps he is diseased. Who knows what diseases he carries with him? He is an outcast. You need crimes at your back to arrive at such a place in such a condition.

Listen to me Liano, he is laden with sins.

He is not for you. I am yours.

Don't you understand? Don't you remember?

We are a natural complement of souls. We are blood and love.

There is no need to seek further.

He will sap you, exhaust you.

Look at yourself!

The effort to retrieve him has almost killed you.

Leave him be. Leave him to me.

I will take him to the centre of the garden.

It will be a quick end and he will quietly rot into the vigour of some beautiful plant.

Believe me, daughter, he has nothing to offer you.

Come. Come to me.

Now that I look at the body I think maybe he's already dead. Maybe she just wants to play with it. As a child she was always curious. It is only natural that she would want to examine a grown man's body at close quarters. I have nothing against her tinkering with it in this way. Once she strips it down and pokes around a little, she'll tire of it quickly enough. This is the way her mind works. I know my daughter.

Olan moved up behind some bushes. As she did so she saw the stiff hood fall from over his face and his mouth opened in a sharp intake of breath. Mechanically her hand tightened on the sword. Now she

had no other choice. Her decision made, whole limbs of trees began
to crack and fall off.

As Liano neared the turret she looked around, baring her teeth.
Olan could see she was trying to figure out how to get the body
upstairs. The dead weight was going to be a problem in her exhausted
condition. Liano was at an incredible pitch of tension and fear. Her
eyes darted from side to side, her actions were clean and immaculate.
Not an ounce of energy was uselessly expended. She opened the
netting and pulled the cushions from around the man's body. Insects
immediately swarmed onto his face, clustering around the pus seeping from his sores. Olan looked at him thinking, his pain must be
delicious and limitless.

He wants to die. Can't you see that, daughter. My ugly daughter.
My weak daughter. He wants to die. Kill him.

Liano bent down to clasp the man underneath his armpits. Olan
saw her chance. In a burst of almost lethal energy she charged from
her point of cover. All sound in the garden suddenly stopped. In that
vacuum of soundless time Olan covered the ground between herself
and Liano, sword held aloft. Liano saw her before she got to the man
and managed to block the downward thrust of the sword. In another
movement she yanked it out of her mother's hand and watched as it
fell some yards away among a clump of bushes. With her head down
Olan rammed into Liano's stomach winding her and throwing her
onto the ground.

'Why are you doing this Liano? He will destroy everything.'

Liano tried to wrestle out of the hold but her arms were pinned down.

'He's no threat, mother. When he's recovered he'll leave of his own
accord. There's nothing here to keep him. Three or four weeks,
mother, and he'll be gone.'

Olan grabbed Liano's hair.

'He's just like Eighad. I have only to look at him to know.'

With a tremendous effort Liano loosened her left hand and hit Olan
on her breast, at the same time bringing her knee up into her groin.
The shock was enough to allow Liano to reverse positions and take

hold of a large rock. She pummelled her mother's face until blood flowed from her ears and mouth. Leaving Olan unconscious she returned to the man. Once again she tried to lift him.

She climbed the circular stairwell slowly with her back against the wall, dragging the body step by step. Once inside Eighad's old room, she pulled him onto the bed, moistened his mouth and returned her thoughts to Olan. For a moment she appeared overwhelmed. She saw no other choice for herself but to put her mother back in the cage. She was more hesitant about doing so than she had been seven months previously since she believed another period of incarceration might kill her. She didn't want to kill her. She rationalised it by telling herself it would last only as long as the man was unable to defend himself.

Olan was still unconscious when Liano returned her to the cage. Opening a vial of salts she brought her round. It was some time before Olan realised where she was. When she did, a stream of invective poured out of her.

'Don't you realise what you're doing?

It's not me should be in here but him.

What do you really want to do?

Watch his member grow between your legs?

Well go ahead. Satisfy your curiosity.

But tell me what are you going to do with him then?'

'Mother it's only for a short while.

I don't want to do this but I can't take any risks.

When he's gone I'll let you out again.'

'He's the risk. Do you think he's going to go when he sees what we have here? A tide of bastards'll come in his wake. Our home will be destroyed.'

Olan was hysterical.

'Mother, he's not like the rest, I can sense it. He'll not betray us.'

'He is a man, daughter. He is the same as Eighad.'

Olan shivered involuntarily and moved to the far end of the cage. Liano had the sudden impulse to enter the cage and comfort her. She felt irresolute, confused and already weary at the prospect of what lay ahead of her. For a long while they remained together in the room. The silence was finally broken by Olan.

'Liano,' she said quietly. 'It is not too late. Take him back for all our sakes. He will not be happy here. What do you have to offer him? You are ugly. I don't mean to demean you but think about it for a moment. Your idea in restoring this man is to have him for yourself. I understand that but remember he may not want you even after you do everything you can for him. When he is fit he may look at you and reject you. He'll reject your body and trample your spirit. Is that what you want? It's not simply a question of a series of kindnesses being rewarded with love. I did not bring you up to be that simple-minded. I am older and have some memory of my past. I ask you now, Liano, before he defiles you, kill him. If you are afraid to do it with a knife I will describe a potion to give him. He will slip effortlessly away.'

Liano was silent. She appeared preoccupied.

Olan continued.

'Liano, you are still beautiful to me.'

Olan could see how frail a creature her daughter really was.

'We must remain faithful to each other. When I saw the man's sores I knew he was diseased. He is an outcast because of his disease. They are plague blisters Liano, I have seen them before. You will be infected within days.'

Liano began to move away.

Olan screamed at her. 'He'll infect you within days. You'll both be dead and then what? What good will it have been? It's not fair to me. Kill him, Liano. Kill him.'

When Liano returned to the tower she felt moody and depressed. Although she had sloughed off her mother's words she suspected they contained a measure of truth. After all, his status as outcast had a source but as yet she could only guess at what it might be. She knew there were dangers inherent in the restorative actions she was about to perform. What if Olan was right and the sores on his body were those of the plague? What if her actions were the axis on which the ultimate destruction of their lives turned?

Standing under the massive lintel of the north tower she knew she could always just leave, lock the door, turn and walk away. His spirit would quietly relinquish its hold and his flesh rot on the clean linen within days. She would recall him as a version of her father who had passed on years before and whose death chamber had become a Holy Sepulchre. Both men would merge into one and she would remember the event as a fateful synthesis, where time had collapsed, where she was a young girl again bearing witness to her father's final hours.

At another point in her life Liano could have conceded her mind to such a delusion, but not now. Her motives, at least on the surface, were, she believed, magnificently uncomplicated. She wanted to see this life saved. She considered herself neither capable nor willing, either through neglect or violent action, to kill him. What she perceived as a surge of bountiful and irrepressible goodness made only the saving of this life a possibility. She had promised him to life when she touched him in the desert and to life she would deliver him.

Liano climbed the stairs of the tower and entered the room. A shaft of sunlight poured down on the man's body. She drew a screen in front of this artery of light and the body was absorbed in shade.

On the table to the right of the bed she placed a selection of knives and scissors, two large bowls, a cluster of small vials filled with herbs, some carrot poultices and a container of pulped fruit. On her way to the tower she had stopped in the kitchen to boil a large cauldron of water and to cut squares of gauze and lengths of cotton which she needed for bandages.

Placing the implements in one bowl she filled both with measures of steaming water. The look and feel of the steel objects had never impressed her more than at this point. They seemed animated by an anticipatory intensity, aware perhaps of their opportunity to shred and redefine this man. Liano took the largest of the scissors, its long shears glimmering in the half light, and slowly began to cut through the soiled and blood-stained robe. The man remained in a stupor throughout the course of her operations which at times were torturously slow. Large areas of the robe had stuck or dried onto the open wounds of his body. The larger gashes still emitted sticky oxidations of green pus. Those parts to which the cloth still adhered, she bathed in a warm solution of water and chervil. Fresh flows of blood occurred with the removal of scab tissue. These she stemmed with bruised borage leaves and powdered peach bark which she sprinkled into the pit of the wound.

From the time Liano had first decided to salvage the man, her mind had begun to retrieve and access her knowledge of remedies necessary for his recuperation. These were derived, in earlier times, from Olan, and partly from manuscripts still extant in the study rooms of the west wing. She was now familiar with a wide range of applications and solutions.

Working through the afternoon she cut the robe from his body, bathed him, bandaged his legs, and spread oils, gums and balm over his skin.

She moved back and forth between the kitchen and the tower replenishing her volume of boiling water or restocking vials with particular herbs and oils. She rubbed the soles of his calloused feet with lemon, then strapped them with cloves of garlic tied with corn silk so that it would infuse through his whole body. She dampened his brow and lips continuously, occasionally raising his head and making him swallow a little. Taking another set of shears she cut his matted and infested head of hair down to the scalp. With a switchblade sharpened on a thong of leather she removed his two weeks growth of beard. Over his bare head and face she spread a milk resin, to cool him and reduce his temperature.

She worked unceasingly throughout the day to effect as great a change in him as possible, to rectify him and make him comfortable. She treated him with great gentleness and by dint of her labours gained an intimacy with his body and spirit which bonded her to him. By nightfall she was exhausted but there was also a feeling of wellbeing within herself, a feeling that for the first time she valued someone's life at least as much as she did her own. She realised now that she had little or no concern for her own safety, her mission was to restore this man to the world and to take full pride in that rehabilitation. It occurred to her that the zeal which now inspired her was similar to that which had provoked her to reclaim the garden. At some level she began to feel that by healing the man she would also heal herself.

In the course of her cleansing and anointing Liano came across the few possessions Hadge had with him. These amounted to a rough map which was crumpled in his fist, a compass, a notebook and a rib. She opened the book and found her father's name inscribed. It was virtually empty. She read what there was carelessly, picking out words here and there, allowing them to conjoin or not with her own ancient version of the past. In the end all she took from her reading was that her father had ventured out in a great storm and never come back. Woven through his description was a disturbing portrait of her mother. Liano closed the book and held it to her heart. The very fact of the book seemed to validate her actions. The man was a link with her father, a messenger of sorts. All of her actions now appeared as though they had been ordained by a higher power, and the placement of this man, whoever he was, in Eighad's old room, was not merely coincidental. In all of this there was the domination of good, things were righting themselves, arranging themselves in a new order. Liano felt light, a lightness of spirit making her feel elevated, free.

As night fell Liano set up some rugs and pillows on the far side of the room. In the course of the night she found herself so attuned to his presence that at the slightest hint of anguish, whether in the difficulty of his breathing or in his need for water, she woke instantly.

In the days that followed Liano watched over him closely, becoming anxious as his fever rose, fretting that she might lose him, willing him with all her might to fight and not relinquish his hold. She tried new poultices and infusions when the fever continued, all to no avail. On the third day the fever broke, his skin lost the pallor of death and his body seemed to indicate a stabilisation of sorts. She cleaned and dressed some of the wounds and changed the bedding which was wet after what was his first urinary release in days.

By mid-morning his condition had worsened again. His skin faded to a jaundiced yellow and he lay in a cramped position holding his stomach. Liano went immediately to prepare a remedy of powdered sunflower seeds mixed into a decoction of sanicle root to increase his urine flow and thus reduce the build up of toxins. A secondary compound of yerba mate and white oak was given in the late afternoon. For the rest of the day he writhed spasmodically in pain. Liano stayed with him throughout. When his whole body shook she cradled him in her arms. Finally exhausted by the ordeal she fell by his side with his hand in hers.

Frequently during this period Liano spoke to the man, comforting him, explaining the nature of her remedies, telling him of how she had come to find him and of the place to which she had carried him. Even though he made no response she felt the inflection of her voice soothed him and conditioned him subconsciously to it. When he wakes, she told herself, he will know my voice and above all others deem it precious.

I stand over him like a sentinel trying to gauge whether his will is great enough to move against this sickness. I ask myself over and over whether there is any more I can do. I am not a practised healer, everything I know I learned from Olan.

Sometimes I think he senses me, by a pressure of his hand in mine, by a mumbling when I mop his brow or cleanse his wounds. Every day I believe he grows stronger. I don't deny that he is becoming more and more beautiful to me. Even though his body is racked by fevers I cherish it above all others. I tell him this. I whisper in his ear that he is beautiful and that I want him to live. Be strong I tell him. I try to instill in him the kind of desire I imagine he needs to survive the complications of this illness.

Sometimes I feel so tired I cannot distinguish one day from another. My hours are differentiated only by the number of times I walk the well-trodden route between the tower and kitchen, boiling water, making poultices, bruising leaves. Yesterday, in order to rid the room of smells, I burned a bowl of frankincense. It seemed to make him sleep more easily.

Often I speculate on what his first words to me will be. Perhaps he knows who I am and all that has occurred. I know there is nothing to fear from this man. Without having spoken to him, I am prepared to entrust him with my life. I feel in a way that I have divined his essence and that he will not hide the truth of himself from me. We will be strong and vulnerable with each other.

When I try to explain how I feel, I find I cannot, or at least not exactly. It is like an intense elation. I have the desire to run for miles and miles in the desert under the sun. I do not want to be hindered by anything, neither by clothes nor walls, but feel the wind on my face and the warm sand beneath my body. When I look around everything appears aerated and fresh. Nothing intrudes in a malicious way. Good has been ladled over all life.

The only obstacle in the fulfilment of my vision is mother. Much as though I want to forget her, I cannot. I am obliged to go to her. I resent this. I resent any time spent away from the man. She would not understand this. Today when I saw her I thought to myself, she is beginning to deteriorate.

Her skin looks as though it's flecked with mould. I feel responsible for her but I cannot risk her release. I tell her this. I explain that she will be freed as soon as the man has recovered and gone on his way. I tell her he is of no interest to me. All she asks is that she be taken out for a turn in the garden each day. Initially I agreed to this but find I have no time to spare for such indulgences.

Two days ago I acceded to mother's demands for make-up and other paraphernalia. Now I find she has thrown most of them beyond the cage. Broken bottles lay strewn about the floor, dyes and other liquids have streaked the walls or clotted on powders. There are clumps and dribbles of various creams accreting on the ceiling. The whole place stinks. As if this wasn't enough she has taken off all her clothes and painted her body. She looks grotesque. The applications have been crude and, together with the ankle bracelets and bells, make her look and sound like a wild animal. She has lost control of herself. This surprises me. I tell her that I would not keep her in such conditions if I could trust her. I ask her whether there is any good reason why I should trust her. She does not answer. Her silence vindicates me. She understands that I have no choice.

When I stand in the shadows and gaze at her, she looks like some strange tribal ghost, her body maroon and crimson. I feed on her with my eyes. When she talks to me one insult follows another. She calls me ugly and regurgitates instances of my stupidity. She says that even if the man revives, his meat will not rise for me. I am protected from these insults by the insistent goodwill I bear everything, even my mother. When I turn to go she cries out, repeating the promises I made. I look at her with what I imagine she perceives as a mixture of condescension and pity and find myself thinking of ways to lessen the time I spend with her.

I have increased the store of food available to her and placed a vat of fresh water within reach of the cage. I find the problem of re-stocking these supplies even on a weekly basis, enormously tedious.

What is it about mother that makes her so unyielding?

Can she not fathom my needs, or having fathomed them believe that they have not been previously fulfilled by her? She believes that we are irrevocably bonded, that too much has passed between us, that because of the nature of our familiarity there can be no one else. She does not understand that what I am doing is part of a necessary series of actions which will take me beyond her points of reference, these actions will formulate the rite of myself in someone else. Even if the man dies I will have an alternative memory to mother. I will have known someone other than her.

Is it too early to say that he cares for me? I know he does. This is not a story to comfort myself. I honestly sense a strength of feeling for me in his blood. He thrives on me. He would not have survived without me, will not survive without me. All of this informs his sleeping mind. Already I can feel indivisible bonds bind us. Soon love will dress us with one robe.

For almost a week now I've slept but little. Still there is no change.

He sleeps continuously and does not seem to be aware of my presence. Occasionally he talks or shouts from the depths of his subconscious mind but there is never enough to piece together a story. Mostly they are just names, pleas for help or sudden screams thrown out into the darkness like stones. I have done everything I can for him and feel I must now wait for the illness to exhaust itself.

His body's need for large doses of sugared liquid has diminished and by all the indications he is healing quite quickly. The open wounds on his tongue and lips have sealed all but completely and the tongue's colour, although pallid, is close to normal. The jaundice, however, has not abated. I feed him pulped yellow tomatoes in mango juice in an attempt to purify his blood and cleanse his kidneys. He hasn't disimproved but I have no idea how long such an illness takes to run its course. I feel helpless and redundant. Sitting here alone I think, perhaps there is one herb which if given in conjunction with another would alter the nature of his body's response. If I could trust mother I would go to her. This after all is her area of knowledge. My results have always been haphazard.

Every day I rub his body with oils to keep it supple. I turn him on the hour to alleviate body pressure and avoid causing bedsores. It shocks me how thin he is. The shape of each rib can be fingered while a tap on the breastbone produces nothing but the hollowest of echoes.

It has become a habit with me these last days to sit on the bed beside him in the late afternoon when the sun fills the room with a golden light. I allow his head to rest languidly in my lap while I stroke it. Occasionally he opens his eyes but he gives no sense that he truly sees or hears. Sometimes I hum and feel as though the sound is coming from far away; the room echoes the note and moves it around the walls like a taper or current of air. The idea occurs to me that I am wrapping him in a cocoon, a sympathetic turbaning of harmonies which will protect him. I wonder if he will look on me specially, when he sees how I have tried to absorb his pain. I do not help him for this reason alone but it will be a great reward if it comes.

How much like the imagined picture of my father this man is. Tall and lean with a sinewy strength and elegance to his thin lines. He is the essence of what I always imagined father to be, what I always loved. Sitting alone with him I see a future of hugs and kisses stretch out in front of me.

When he is well I will take him into the desert. I will take him to places that are important to me, places which I prize and which have a consistent and ancient attraction for me. There I will speak as I have never spoken, embrace as I have never embraced, and in the silent centre of the desert, watch as a host of great lizards encircle us, symbolising the eternity of our commitment.

I practise talking to him and have even gone so far as to give him a name. I call him Eighad in reverence to my father. Perhaps he will adopt this name when he recovers. Sometimes I answer for him. He thanks me for everything and whispers to me that I am beautiful. I let my eyelids fall, embarrassed. He too is shy and doesn't say any more. He takes my hand and with a gentle pressure communicates the full extent of his feeling. My heart is bursting with joy. This is perfect. This is perfection itself. When I leave him I think, tomorrow he will wake and speak to me. My life is full of hope. I am a changed woman.

It's only when I see mother that I am dragged down to base level again. I look at this woman caked in mud and paint and feel that I should be repulsed. Strangely I'm not. I don't understand why. She has become wild and mad. She shakes her body at me and curses me until I think her tongue is going to fall out. She shakes her bottom and tells me to fuck her. I say nothing but I have the sudden and inexplicable urge to rip my clothes off and climb into the cage with her. She makes me feel guilty and violent. She strikes to the core of my dream and plants her own vision. Suddenly I want her to shiver at the end of my fingers. I want to hear her say, 'beat me, daughter. Beat me.' I beat her. It is what she wants. Step by step I move back from the cage. It's like pulling away from some huge force.

Despite the trials of dealing with the man and with mother, I feel stronger in myself than I ever have before. This new level of responsibility and dependency is fortifying. Perhaps it is the attendant increase in the sense of my own worth which is making me more beautiful. When I look in the mirror I notice changes, small changes admittedly but significant nonetheless. The deep craters and scars on my cheeks have fleshed and evened out. The general oiliness of my skin is less and there are fewer pimples than for years past. I have been to Olan's room and taken some perfumes and creams. When I outline my eyes in black the difference is extreme. I have always considered my eyes my most beautiful feature. When they are open the lids are barely visible, they slant upwards very slightly. I have also taken to dressing a little more flamboyantly, sometimes like mother.

Perhaps it is because of these changes and preoccupations that I have begun to push mother into the back of my mind. There have been days recently when I have forgotten about her completely. I remedy this by making the decision to clean her cage. Unfortunately this has become a necessary function and one which I resent doing. She refuses to use the toilet which means her stools, which are often large, litter the straw bedding. Because of the way she throws herself about she is often covered up to her knees in her own waste. It takes an hour at least to accomplish the ablution. When the bedding is removed I throw buckets of lemon water over both mother and the boards of the cage. If straw is in short supply I provide her with banana leaves. Incredibly she will urinate or defecate on boards I have just cleaned. I tell her that if she continues in this way I will stop cleaning the cage altogether. Unless she decides to co-operate no favours will be granted. She tells me to go fuck myself.

With regard to the cage and the mess she makes, I think of possibilities such as cutting down on the rations available to her. If she defecated less it would mean a commensurate decrease in the amount of work I would have to do with the compensating side effect of making her less energetic. I also consider blocking off the window since the light seems to encourage an obsessional streak in her. The other idea which has occurred to me is to introduce some tapeworm eggs into her diet, but this may be an excess I would come to regret.

Yesterday when she saw me dressed in all her finery and smelling so sweetly she screamed.

'Take my clothes off! Take them off!'

Of course she's angry because they make me look pretty. This response encourages me and confirms that I am not self-deluded.

When I return to Eighad's room, that of the old Eighad and the new, I move my pillows closer to the bed so as to be near him at all times. It is my earnest hope at this point that I will be present when he wakes. That I will be standing over him with a loving and concerned look on my face. Witnessing me in this aspect with the sun perhaps flowing in through the window and outlining my figure in a radiant glow, he will see me in the best possible light.

Any day now his eyes will open like julien pods, his feet will root and his body strive upwards towards the light. All of the things I have coveted and desired will spume forth. This whole section of time will culminate in a fantastic scintillation of my life.

Up to now there has been an insistent voice inside me saying, you and Olan are irrevocably dedicated to each other. Had it not been for the man I believe we would have continued along our parallel corridors meeting only to violate each other, our lives enlivened only by the course of ambivalent feeling we bore each other, our simulations and gambits becoming more obscene.

He has distorted this rhythm, his life motions us otherwise.

When I think back on it, Olan and I achieved a kind of numbness through the gradual layering of violences, which eventually worked themselves up to a maelstrom of malfeasance, a world of resistance and degradation. All of that which is so complexly past still binds us, making the pattern of my repetitions perhaps unavoidable. This is my fear.

Mother will never stop intruding, I know that. But perhaps she will remain on the perimeter and not attempt to deny me what is mine. Mother, stay where you are. Trust me. This is what I want. I will shortly have everything I want. Do you understand this repetition? Of course you do. This is your life too. This is a description of the same pattern.

Today when I was sitting with Eighad I began to tell him stories.

Stories of my life here in the Fortress, incidental things which I think he might want to hear. I have not told him about mother. I think it is better that I say nothing for the moment. He would only see it as a problem and perhaps want to do something about it. It would distract his attention. Really I don't want him to have to worry about such things. I have told him I live alone. I say this in a strong voice so as not to appear vulnerable. I tell him he is welcome to stay as long as he wants.

I have planted certain ideas which I hope will have rooted by the time he finally wakes. I have told him that the Fortress is a volatile thing, that it is like me. I have told him that life within the Fortress is out of balance and that he has been sent to rectify it. I tell him that he must not think of leaving, not until his work is accomplished. I tell him he is free to leave at any time. So as to accustom him to me I have described myself, not glowingly but with pride and honesty. It is not in my interest to paint a false picture of myself.

He seems so real and complex to me now that I cannot imagine him answering back in any way other than with the phrases I supplant for him. He tells me unusual things. Not always the things I want to hear but this in a way vouchsafes his honesty. After I clean him I sometimes scent him with oils I have taken from Olan's room. For some reason I don't mind that he smells like Olan. The attraction of her scent on him surprises me. I slip in beside him and we lie side by side looking up at the vaulted ceiling with the late afternoon sunlight filtering in through the window. I turn on my side to look at his face. It is such a beautiful face. Sometimes I see a resemblance between us. I wonder whether we are not beginning to develop a degree of similitude.

When I think I am boring him I read aloud from one of my father's books. The one I have chosen is a history of Hannibal moving with his train of strange animals across the heights of the Alps. I read for hours stopping intermittently to mop his brow or remove one of the bandages which has become sodden with pus or blood.

I have prepared some light broths and fish dishes for when he awakens. I expect him to open his eyes at any moment. I cannot take my eyes off him. I want to be the first thing he sees. I have told him my name many times, giving it a variety of inflections, pulling it this way and that to make it more delicate and appealing. Sometimes I see the corners of his mouth curl up into a smile. Perhaps he thinks it's a game.

It is such a comfort to have someone else to talk to.

— ~ —

He woke today and I wasn't there. I cannot describe my disappointment.

I had gone to replenish mother's water supply. When I returned he was awake. An absence of no more than half an hour. I blame it on her. I am working against making too much of this. After all, who's to say I didn't appear just after he opened his eyes? It's just that I was sure everything was going to be perfect. When I entered the room I was immediately aware of a difference in him. I closed the door firmly so as to announce my presence, to forewarn him. I was trembling as I approached the edge of the bed. I felt like a little girl again trembling before the prepared altar of my mother. This was not a memory or feeling I wanted to indulge so I settled instead on the image of his body, the body I had tended and which I now knew as well as my own. I stood by the side of the bed and waited for him to speak. I did not dare meet his eyes with my own. Was I afraid they would not image my dreamed version of them? How wrong I was. It seemed that I stood for a long time before he spoke. When he did, it was with a question.

'Are you Olan?' he asked.

This was my second disappointment.

I looked at him, appealing to him with my eyes. Don't you remember all that I have told you, they said.

In my gentlest voice I answered him.

'Olan was my mother. My name is Liano.'

At the mention of the name he seemed to remember something. 'Is this the Fortress?'

I nod, unable to speak. His voice is deeper than I expected but very pleasant. I like his voice. I sense a mountain of questions on both sides waiting to be asked, but both of us are wary, trying to find our ground.

'One of my last memories,' he says, 'is of crawling out from under the shadow of Bradaz to a sheep. How did I manage to get here?'

I tell him the story of his rescue, embellishing a little here and there. Images return to him. He remembers, for example, when I stood over him dressed in a red robe. He looks at his body, clean, bandaged and scented and communicates the fact that he owes me a great debt. My whole body tingles with joy.

'How many families are here in the Fortress?'

'There are none. I am the only one left. My mother died some years ago.'

'Are there no other settlers who would wish to live here?'

I answer abruptly so as to discourage this line of questioning. He will realise in time why others steer clear of this ground.

I sit on a small stool by the corner of the bed. I raise him up slightly on pillows. He is still very weak. After all I have said to him in the course of this past week I find I have nothing to say to him now. My tongue is tied. I find myself smiling continuously.

Whenever our eyes meet I blush. I dislike this sensation immensely. I have the sense that he is not happy with what he sees. Olan's words haunt me. I expect him to say something but he says nothing. He appears watchful, guarded, as though he is under threat. I have seen the same look before in animals under sentence. I am becoming nervous. This is not at all how I wanted things to go. I begin to shrink down while still pouring spoonfuls of broth into his mouth. He is silent. I try to think back to the conversations I had with him before he woke. Which questions elicited the greatest response? I consider these. In this atmosphere they appear meaningless. I say nothing. I decide I must look at him with courage. I do. For the first time his eyes appear dark and kind. Although it is obviously painful for him he tries to smile at me. His features animate and alter the whole design of his face.

I try to shed my fear and ask him what I want to know.

'How did you come to be lost in the desert?'

He turns his head. His look is inquisitorial. He hesitates as though he does not want to tell me. I can see him gauge the range of my fears.

'How far are we from Limbah?' he asks.

Is this an answer or is he already planning a route of escape?

'I've never been but I've heard it's twelve to fifteen days travel in good conditions. Have you to go there?'

'No.'

His eyes lose their focus. I can see him cataloguing memories.

Silence.

When he returns his eyes to me, he tells me the story of the woman and of his escape. I find his escapade exciting but am worried about his relationship with the woman.

'Is she dead?' I ask, perhaps a little too anxiously.

His look is like a judgement.

'I don't know,' he replies, then re-evaluates. 'Yes I suppose she is.'

Mother's admonitions surface again. The reality of the woman's disease pressures the question as to whether or not he is a carrier.

'Sima's ailment,' he says, 'didn't originate with me. However there's the possibility that I am infected.'

The manner in which I receive this information emphasises the depth of my humanitarianism. I am proud of my strength.

He tells me of his journey into the desert.

'I was making for the eastern caravan route which I thought was fifty miles or so north north east of Limbah. A storm threw me off course which is how I came upon the grave of your father.'

He looks around as though remembering something.

'Where is the rib?'

I go to a table at the far end of the room and retrieve his belongings. As I hand them to him he realises the oddness of the situation. He confides to me that the rib was like a spiritual marker for him, in a way it was his salvation. He hands it back to me.

This sequence of words and actions is recorded by me as our first real communication.

After a long silence I volunteer the fact that I never knew my father. He and my mother had a complex relationship. For years my mother led me to believe that he left shortly before my birth and went to live with a woman from the Jabodin tribe in one of the northern towns.

Holding the rib in my hands stimulates the sense of a unique connectedness between us. We are united by my father. I ask him if he will take me to the grave when he is recovered. He promises to do so. Already I can feel the layers of a personal history build up around us.

Sometimes when I catch him off guard I can see a distracted look in his eyes as though his physical surroundings are part of a mystery he cannot fathom. Sometimes I have the feeling that he is trying to reconcile himself to the fact that he is not dead. By turns his eyes are aimless and startled. He does not say it but I know that he had conditioned himself to death.

He is still very weak. He looks exhausted after this, our first conversation. I remove the pillows at his back and resettle him in the bed. Before leaving I ask him his name.

'Hadge,' he says.

On closing the door I say to him, 'Rest now, Hadge.'

I reflect that this has not been a perfect beginning but nonetheless I feel happy.

—— ~ ——

He improves day by day and continues to sleep much of the time. When I change his dressings I sometimes allow my hand to rest gently on his flesh as a caress. Occasionally I sense his muscles tighten when I do this, other times he seems to welcome it. I feel confused and want to be with him every minute of the day.

He has made it clear to me that I should go about my business, that I should conduct myself as I would normally. Doesn't he understand my needs? Is this his way of declining my attentions? Were it not that he communicates his uneasiness at being a patient, maintaining that he does not want to place extraordinary demands on me, I would feel aggrieved, depressed. As it is I expand and feed off these sensitive reproaches and stay away from him as much as possible.

Today he seemed very much alive although his kidney and liver problems persist. I have kept him on the yellow tomato and mango diet which seems to be doing him some good. He has lost the yellow pallor of jaundice and says only that there is some pain during urination. He asks me about the Fortress. I try to describe it as best I can but find it difficult. I have told him about the garden. I have to catch myself from slipping into the we, mother and me. She still swims annoyingly in my head, creating a tension which I fear is tangible. He has asked me again if I am alone. I insist that I am. He questions me about my mother, about my recollections of her, about her recollections of my father. I find such questions and conversations extraordinary. They are totally alien to me. No one of course has asked me about my parents in the way he does. He leads me into new areas. I enjoy being interrogated in this manner. It excites me. Everything about this man excites me. I am being challenged to recall and create a past on the spot. When I am alone now, I find myself adding more details to my story. I lead him quietly into areas of my life and unfold my latest fabrications.

Whenever we talk about his recovery I leave him in no doubt that he has a place to stay. He smiles. His gums and teeth are looking more healthy. Yesterday I provided him with a larger chamber pot for his use. I take the pot away each morning and empty it. Since I introduced solids into his diet his stools have taken on a more regular shape. Their texture and smell have become less weak and offensive. I have taken to mixing them with my own and burying them under the roots of sunflowers.

When I entered the room today he was standing by the window.

It was impossible for him, however, to achieve any sense of the garden, obscured as it is by the dense grove of date palms just beyond the tower.

I try to become more sophisticated in my responses. His questions test me, pressing me to use my mind. I enjoy this opportunity to make myself over, to re-create myself in a more appealing way, to be according to a desired alternative. I attempt to pit myself against my past and ordain a less troubled version. It is an investiture or an exploration of possibilities, a critical re-assessment of the negative in my spirit. A negativity sublimely linked to the existence of mother. Gradually she is becoming less alive to me. It cannot be otherwise. Whether at some point I present her to the man is open to doubt. It depends on how satisfied he is with life here. But I don't want to think about that now. I am too happy.

— ~ —

In the large circular room of the north tower Hadge lay stretched out on the tapestried cover of the bed. He guessed it was early morning by the quality of light which poured in through the window at the far end of the room, illuminating the series of paintings to which he had gradually grown accustomed. He had slept well and felt refreshed, more like his old self again.

When he thought back over the weeks that had passed he felt vindicated by the mere fact of his survival. There was a real sense of his having been delivered from death, of having been secured fatefully according to a coda he couldn't fathom. Images of the past few days returned to him with a visionary distillation. The most potent of these was his first impression of Aganatz. In that interlude of alertness on the journey to the Fortress he had seen the great white indented battlements with the hint of an extravagant verdure floating against a backdrop of intense blue sky. These images persisted in a kind of oasis of consciousness surrounded on all sides by the stupor which had enveloped him. There was one other detail from his reconnaissance of the battlements which niggled in his memory but which he could not retrieve. It would come or not, in time, and he did not press himself.

As he looked around the room he still occasionally suspected the tenure of its reality. Was this sequence yet another alliance of illusions? After what he'd been through, the sense that the girl and the room were merely mental figments was difficult to override. Still, each day saw an increase in his belief in the propriety of his salvation.

He could still see a length of life he had yet to walk and he was never more aware than now of the irrepressible spirit which strove within him.

Hadge realised of course that the major factor in his survival had been the girl. When he thought of her now his feelings were mixed between those of intense gratitude and natural wariness. He did not fully understand her motivation or her almost aggressive desire to spend as much time as possible in his company. To some extent he distrusted her goodness, her overweening attentiveness, which seemed out of all proportion either to his needs or to that with which he was comfortable. He really did not know what to think of her. He felt vulnerable by his weakness and, partly because of this, distrusted his own judgement of things. He warned himself against being overly hasty in reaching any conclusions about Liano, the Fortress, or indeed anything else he confronted during this period of his recovery.

Hadge saw Liano as solicitous and generous, a young woman who by all accounts had little else to do except cater to his needs. He was suspicious however of her limpet-like attraction but understood that the nature of her isolation might explain the cause of her developing dependency. Initially he had found it hard to credit the truth of her isolation. A Fortress this size, with what he imagined to be a large garden, supporting only one was beyond belief. Occasionally she seemed to express in her look, gesture or speech, the desolateness of her situation, and it was at such times that he saw no contradiction between what she said and what he still suspected to be the truth.

This suspicion that there was a cunning manipulation of details stemmed in part from the fact that he had noticed discrepancies in her conversation, stories of her childhood which did not match from day to day, or did in substance but not in tone. Again, at such an early stage he could not put his finger on it, but he felt that something was awry.

Although Liano had made it clear to him from the start that he was welcome to stay, he remained tight lipped about his intentions. Privately he tried to gauge how long it would be before the wounds on his legs healed and his system felt sufficiently restored to contemplate a journey south. He had no intention of remaining at the Fortress. With supplies he could make it to Doan and from there to the Gulf. Even at this early stage he began to work on his itinerary and with pencil and paper made an initial list of what he might need.

As he continued to sit, propped up by cushions and pillows, he stared through the large window thirty or so feet beyond the foot of the bed, recording the events which had led him first to the grave and then to the Fortress, where he now slept in the dead man's bed, among his paintings and books. He felt as though there had been a synapse of time, with the intervening years between Eighad's death and his own salvation, squeezed as though to nothing. There was the inescapable sense of some ancient course being followed, an inevitable rotation of events which was turning still and which would lead him he knew not where. Were spirits tampering with his life, dead souls gaining access and making of him an instrument? Was he being goaded to vacate his will and allow a ghostly interference to manage his blood? He could only remain vigilant and not concede to the kind of paranoia this sequencing of events might induce.

When he had spoken to Liano during the preceding few days he had probed her about her relationship to her mother. It sounded more of a conjured memory than anything else, which to Hadge was understandable, given that she had been dead for thirteen years. The story which emerged was that Olan had died of boar wounds in the garden when Liano was about twelve. Liano's memories of her mother were vague and dispassionate. With regard to contact with travellers she said there was none. She gave a plausible explanation of why both the Fortress and its inhabitants were seen as an evil formulation. She communicated the difficulty inherent in her decision to save Hadge at all. Again he expressed his gratitude for the risk she had taken.

As the days passed, their daily actions became more ritualised. Each morning she brought him an earthenware bowl full of steaming water, a block of scented soap and the leather case containing Eighad's old razor. She liked to sit on the edge of the bed holding the mirror as he stripped the lather off in clean swipes. After shaving him Liano would check his wounds and bandages. Most of the smaller surface wounds had healed with the scabs beginning to flake off, while those on his shins and the soles of his feet were no longer infected. After treating him she washed his body down with warm rosewater then rubbed in a variety of oils. Hadge felt like a cherished object and, try as he might, he could not get her to temper the lavishness of her attentions. At times he found the casualness of her familiarity with his body annoying, but the lack of embarrassment or awkwardness on her part made it easier for him to submit to her hands.

The movement of both their lives was simple and uncluttered. Liano would occasionally spend the day herding the sheep to new pastures or tending to one or other part of the garden. She left Hadge alone as much as possible, to read or as he increasingly did these days, to write. The effect of these last weeks on Hadge was to promote a meditative and reflective bias. It was as though he had been gifted with new eyes and was seeing from that point in life when the coin flips and the tail-side of significant pain is experienced and ultimately valuated as good. The experience of these last weeks was one of utter and complete collapse, but it was an experience which had forwarded its own humanising reward. He could now see with the eyes of the truly delivered.

He returned to his past and began to assess the course of his life.

Up to now he had been a wanderer, an intellectual vagrant, moving up and down the coast, stopping for periods, involving himself in issues and communities but consistently moving on. Now he was in the middle of nowhere and instinctively he felt at home. In its very isolation Aganatz seemed like an empathetic structure, a physical reflection in some ways of how he conceived of himself, sturdily entrenched in a wasteland not only of ideas but of human relationships. He continued to work on the itinerary for his journey south but more and more he believed that a short sojourn in Aganatz might provide him with the time to focus his ideas, interrogate his past and determine his desires.

When Liano came to him that evening with a meal of rice and curried fruit, he looked at her, truly looked at her and he understood that love roved though her whole system. She was both light and substantial. At times she seemed to glide over the flagstones in the room, yet, when he saw her from behind, there was a beautiful massiveness to her buttocks and a sumptuous arch in the curve of her back. In fact he began to have the sense of her beauty ripening before his eyes, as if she had sourced the current of her own sensuality and was allowing it to flow through her blood and into her pores.

Gradually he found himself becoming attracted to her, attracted primarily perhaps by her love for him, by her loving indulgence, by her selflessness. There began to exist between them a state of seductive compatibility. Now when her fingers touched his skin there was the sense that he finally recognised the nature of her desire and by the quality of his touch communicated his willingness to reciprocate.

After twenty-eight days Hadge's wounds were sufficiently healed and he prepared himself to take his first steps outside the room. Liano had suggested they go to the small room at the top of the tower. From that vantage point, she promised, Hadge could achieve a sense of the garden and of the surrounding panorama. He desperately craved the refreshment of pure air and wanted to fill his eyes with a demesne of sky. He had been entombed for too long.

On the morning of his proposed walk Liano came and breakfasted with him. She brought a cane of polished tamarisk capped in silver. It had been Eighad's and still bore his initials inscribed below the rim. Liano was in high spirits. Over the past few days she had found herself doing things which previously would have seemed alien to her character. Her love for Hadge had become a demonstrable thing, she wanted to be with him at all times, to touch him, to whisper, solicit and cajole him. The conditional terms by which she had always lived her life with Olan had vanished. She was in a mood of loving indulgence. The physical changes which had begun with Hadge's arrival at the Fortress now continued. Her body lines had become fluid and fulsome and day by day she seemed to lose the bony angularity and scrawniness which was a relic of an old neurosis, of a dissuasive image of herself. Love had become a kind of soporific for her, she relished its heat and was reformed by its ability to simplify the complex habit of things. This feeling was at the centre of life and motivated all that was good, and selfishly she wanted to protect her source and make it last. Each action concealed or disclosed love's promise, each word was a flowering of love's intent.

Liano did not fully understand the process by which she had been claimed by love. She felt deliciously vulnerable, disarmed. Most of all she felt discovered. Finally someone had noticed her. The fact of its absence in her life up to then only increased her need for the very succour she was beginning to find with Hadge. Here was someone who responded to her and was profoundly obliged to her.

Now at last, she thought, my life has begun.

With the cane in his left hand and his right arm around Liano's shoulders, Hadge moved away from the bed. The room was in deep shadow with only an angled band of sunlight sectioning the lower end of the room from window to door. Although his legs were weak he felt invigorated at the prospect of finally moving beyond the room.

Outside the door was a broad spiral staircase. Climbing slowly they eventually came to the uppermost chamber. The room was small and completely bare. A glass orb covered the dome allowing through a plenitude of light, stimulating an atmosphere of intense airiness and

elevation. The circular walls were lime-washed and partly discoloured. An arched wooden door led out to a slated balustrade.
Hadge moved out, propped himself against the stone guard and
looked down. He felt dizzy. The drop he gauged to be about two
hundred feet. What he looked out on almost defied credibility. The
word garden seemed to him a mere euphemism for what was an
outlandishly textured tropical arena. It was its vastness which awed
him most. To the south and west rose up great forests and craggy
elevations, plantations of broad-leaved trees partly occluded by hot
vapours. To the east a grass plain led down to orchards, ornamental
plots of manicured hedges and a smaller section of tilled acreage.
Close to the centre was an expanse of water with flotations of giant
lily pads visible even at this distance. The garden communicated a
sense of frenetic jostling activity, a vigorous kingdom of oppressively
extravagant flowers and plants. It was a storehouse of great bounty
with the trees bent to the weight of outsized ripening fruit.

The day was brilliantly clear with the sun's heat uncorrupted by
cloud or diminished by wind. Turning around Hadge looked out on
the desert. The sand's normally dun colour had lightened and with
the sun dazzling his eyes seemed to transform into an extensive white
plain. Hadge breathed in deeply. As he relaxed and conditioned
himself to this somewhat precarious perch he marvelled at the landscape below him. To the south he could see the great rock of Bradaz
rise up in dramatic isolation with the desert sweeping away on all
sides. The sight of it revived his initial perception of its strangely
animate qualities.

The terrain between Bradaz and Aganatz gave way to dune
clusters and what appeared to be stone islands comprised of large
boulders. In the background the Kalakut mountains under which
Limbah nestled, described a ragged outline. Looking south Hadge
asked Liano the direction of Doan.

The question was disconcerting in its abruptness and hinted at a
scenario Liano had no wish to entertain, but rather than prejudice him
against her she lifted her arm and pointed south south west.

Liano preceded him down the steps of the tower and into the room. After settling him on the bed she left him to rest.

During the days that followed Hadge became preoccupied with the garden and the Fortress. He was fascinated and intrigued by both and was keener than ever to explore this strange settlement. Encouraged by the prospect of what lay ahead, his body energised itself, reclaiming an old suppleness and power.

Liano had made some new garments for him and mended the best remnants of Eighad's wardrobe. For his feet she had made two pairs of thick felted slippers. Hadge was delighted with the gifts and kissed her in thanks. Liano had never been so content.

On the morning that he first walked out from under the shadowed arch of the great tower, the light was sullen and the pavestones damp after what had been a brief though violent storm. The garden reeked of a fern root aroma and the plants appeared newly pulsed by the sustaining fall of rain.

Directly in front of the tower, Hadge found himself facing a plantation of large palms the base of whose trunks were covered in fibrous growths. To his right stretched a wide gravel path with bamboo fields on the inner side. Branch pathways led off towards the centre of the garden. The density of the plant life was imposing and claustrophobic, the heat at this ground level cloying and stultifying. Taking the red cloth Liano had given him, he wiped his forehead and followed her down the sloping pathway. Looking up he saw flocks of birds gathered in the canopy. He hadn't realised how much insulation the room had provided. Here in the garden or at least in this section the noise of the birds was overwhelming and made conversation difficult.

Moving along the western flank, away from the date plantation, they passed an area fertile with large tube flowers. These rose upwards to thirty feet on thick cylindrical stems with only the upper ten feet putting out leaves. Shooting out at the top was a poker-like cluster of red berries. The plants appeared to be aberrant versions of ones he had seen before but he could not be certain. The air was now pungent with the scent of broken vanilla pods.

Thirty minutes steady walking had still not brought them to the end of the western side. The heavier pubescent stems thinned out for periods giving way to shrub growths and giant docks. Hadge glimpsed herds of tusked boars together with some larger animals among the deeper recesses of the inner garden. He understood now why Liano had made him carry the long spear tipped pole, telling him it was a necessary precaution.

The Fortress itself was made of cut blocks of white stone, its windowed and balconied facades facing onto the garden. Along the west side Hadge noted two main entrances with numerous side doors which Liano explained led to store-rooms and cellars. She told him that a system of underground tunnels spread in spoke-like formation out into the desert. Although never having investigated them herself, her mother had told her as a child that those which had not collapsed were infested with vermin.

After passing a putrid plot of seeding sunflowers Hadge stepped briefly inside one of the two main entrances. It opened into a large blue vestibule with a vaulted ceiling on which ran a circularly in-scribed pattern. The walls were painted in the same grey-cobalt base, with the last application appearing to have been an ancient one. Towards the back of the vestibule, which extended for perhaps one hundred feet, was a stone stairwell which was in deep shadow. To the right and left were two broad corridors. He could not positively discern an end to these due primarily, he believed, to the quality of the light. The wall appeared to blur and waver as its course tapered. The stone had a fluctuous, moveable essence which gave the impres-sion of a permutating structure. Walking a short distance down the left hand corridor he found smaller channels and arteries, branching off to what were variously, voluminous and tiny rooms. Not one possessed a stick of furniture to connote occupation.

Although Hadge had seen but a small section of one wing the idea of replicating it by four made him feel as though he was in the centre of a huge structural maze with an infinitely complex body system of connecting passageways, and that this was matched and multiplied on each of the four stories of each wing, and that all were circuitously linked.

Liano's contention, that after all her years in the Fortress, there were still areas she had yet to investigate, was now comprehensible to him. She also commented on the dangers of walking within the ambit of the Fortress without her as guide. There was a sense of proscription in her explanation. Hadge said nothing but privately decided to explore as he wished when the opportunity presented itself.

Walking back into the garden they came to plants whose life terms were virtually instantaneous. Standing beside them he watched as they grew, blossomed, seeded and died. Other areas were held in states of perpetuity, as though they had continued to grow at a certain pace for thousands of years. This seam of ancientness was a perceptible manifestation, more in the texture of their leaves and the cork-like quality of their stems than in their size. There were a number of other sections which contained these outlandish extremes and juxtapositions.

Hadge followed Liano at a short distance, the scroop of her silk dress drawing his eyes to the motivating movement of flesh underneath. With the sun now beginning to break through disbanding clouds he felt the sap rise in him as of old. He examined this lustful factor and realised it as part of a progression. Their relationship up to this point had followed a strange route. There were intimacies to be sure, familiarities, but as yet no passion. He had in the main warded her off, presented himself on an inner level as an untouchable essence, feeling the need to gather himself, sensing that if the physical impulse were surrendered to, it would only fragment him further. He saw the spawning growth of the garden as a pivotal element in the resurgence of his blood, goading him now to test the fertility of her physical feeling for him.

Among a grove of nut trees along the southern side Liano led him by the hand in towards the centre which was an intense sun-filtered arena of variegated greens. From the boughs of the trees hung glass vials, filled with what Liano told him was her own menstrual blood, most of which had compacted and dried to the sides of the tubes over time. She showed him the deposit of her most recent flow, it too had thickened and blackened in the heat and seemed to have a ferrous tinge to it. In a far corner were four discoloured vials with cabbage coloured scales flecking the sides. These, he was told, were Eighad's. Recognising a coincidence of intentions Hadge pressured his body to her, their bodies communicating a complex transference of emotion. Shadowed in half-light he cupped her face with his hands and kissed her lips.

Opening her top Liano encouraged him to touch her breasts. Drawing her down onto a cushion of moss he slipped the silk off her shoulders, whispered his mouth over her breasts, massaging the tip of one and then the other with his tongue. Liano straddled him, with her legs high up along the sides of his chest. In a series of succulent dips backward she fostered her softened centre over him, allowing the head of his penis to push slowly and deeply within her. He came almost immediately.

They remained entwined together, holding, caressing. Both felt subsumed, integrated.

Now at last, thought Liano, I am truly loved.

Rousing themselves they walked out onto the pathway and down a slight hill. By late afternoon they had reached the mid-point of the southern end. Rather than continue along the perimeter Liano told him she would take him in towards the centre to the pond. The route they took was one of those Liano had cleared the previous winter during her mother's incarceration. She was both surprised and disappointed by the extent to which the dramatic impact of her clearances had been dissolved by the burgeoning growth of these unstable plants. Still, access was a simple enough matter along the main pathway.

Hadge found substantial differences between this inner path and those running close to the Fortress walls. Sunlight was an occasional source, with the overlapping canopy blocking all but the weakest threads of light. This dark lower zone resembled a burnt out shrubland with the lowest branches having all but withered. Parasitic mosses and lichens massed on the trunks and on the ground spread a dense layer of repulsive ivies and wax myrtles. This oppressive contusion of darkness only began to be relieved when Hadge caught sight of the numerous irrigation channels fanning out from the mono-lithic wood wheel churning under a surf of water. Weaving through a growth of fern and grass to the accompanying cries of disturbed birds, he gained his first glimpse of the pond. Once again the word was a euphemistic diminution of what from any standpoint was a sizeable expanse of water, broadly circular in shape, with large areas of reeds and lilies forming a continuous surface cover. Moving over a clearing of grass they came to a sloping shale-covered beach. Willow-like boughs fell over the banks and when the water shim-mered for a few seconds Liano pointed to a plait of eels visible just below the surface. The water quickly reclaimed its glass-like simula-tion. Sitting on the upper bank Hadge allowed this even and reposeful scene to fill his head. To his right his eye caught sight of a group of low shrubs whose leaves were mottled yellow. He had seen individ-ual plants with the same discolouration throughout the garden and it was only their intense profusion in this particular spot which attracted his attention. On further investigation many of the leaves were brittle, with black lines on the veins. He asked Liano if she had seen anything like it before or indeed if she knew of a solution to protect the plants. She agreed that it was a disease of some sort but knew neither its origin, nor any way to combat it other than to root out the infected plants and burn them. She told him to wait and see how it developed.

'In a garden of this size,' she said, 'diseases of some sort or another are always running their course.'

Hadge returned to the bank and, with the glow of the late afternoon sun finding its reflection in the water, he felt inwardly calm. He had an overwhelming sense of having reached a point of settlement and agreement, both with himself and with the world. His spirit felt free and keenly responsive within this isolated frame of reference. His passionate relationship to Liano was a beginning, and with it would come the kindling of a deep-seated emotional flare.

Up until a few days previously he had speculated that the Fortress would at best be a facilitator, that within its confines, he could recover, write, and perhaps originate a new course for himself. Now however that he had begun to relax into its atmosphere and condition himself to a new habit of life, he believed that the unities and disunities of his thought might be clarified, ordaining a man of renewed hope and enthusiasm. He had the sense that within the structure of this hermetic retreat, things would be simplified. Good and evil would register with a more brazen emphasis and would provide him with an ideal against which to set what had passed of his life. He would be enriched by this in-dwelling in himself, and perhaps in time, he too might come to call the Fortress home.

Liano stirred him from this reverie and urged him to follow her back along the path before nightfall. It was a sealed darkness which fell, alleviated only by a series of glimmering lamps in the ground floor of the southern wing.

They entered through a large doorway with Liano leading him to a kitchen in the centre of which stood a deal table decked with food. On the high walls of the kitchen hung rows of gleaming pots and pans and an assortment of culinary paraphernalia. Going to a storeroom across the corridor Liano tapped a pitcher of date wine from one of the older casks. The mellowness of the beverage complimented the food and in the sublime atmosphere created by the lamps, they ate and were sated.

Liano went to lie down while Hadge remained.

Still anxious to explore he took one of the lamps and went to the main vestibule.

Walking along a side corridor Hadge passed by a system of rooms each containing volumes of preserves. Stepping inside the third room on the right hand side he found glass jars neatly stacked on stout wooden shelving. On a podium in one corner sat a huge squat container which, unlike the others, bore no label describing its contents.

Examining it he tried to discern through its murky brine the shapes which floated within. He could not. Taking the cap he twisted it. Suddenly in the background he heard the sound of glass shattering, and the wail of a child's scream began to fill the room. He returned the cap to the jar and twisted it tight cancelling the terror.

'Liano,' he called out. But his voice was muted.

The sharded echo of the scream hung in the air.

Further on, he came to a stairs which led downwards. Like every-thing else within the confines of the Fortress it had a moveable quality as though there was a blurring of lines, a myopia of efforts stimulated by the stone. As he descended, flows of water trickled down the grouted blocks of marble. Wetting his fingers he tasted it. Lime was the predominant mineral. The deeper he went the lower became the ceiling until he was crawling backwards on his knees. He would have turned back but it appeared that the stairs had stopped in mid air and all he could perceive was a faded group of vibrating steps. Beneath him the stone had become a soluble mass and he slithered backwards on his belly. He was stopped by a rough mud or calcate wall at the bottom of which was a small opening. Squirming through he knew immediately that he was in a large ventilated chamber. Holding the lamp above his head he could make out some of the details of the cavern and its one remarkable feature. Hanging from the roof was a mountainous stalactite with rivulets of calcate-rich water running in grooves along its cone shape and agglomerating at its tip. Smaller pudge forms had moulded on the ground beneath it.

Looking at it from all sides Hadge realised that it bore an intimate resemblance to the inverted shape of the great granite eruption that was Bradaz. He tried to discredit this notion but each detail he recalled from his period at Bradaz was simulated in the stalactite. Even if this postulation were true there was no reason to be disconcerted by such a reflection. He had partially come to terms with the strangeness of Aganatz and this he rationalised as merely one more manifestation of it. It was a link to the outside world, possibly a twining of images and indicative of a mirror-like tracery he would witness elsewhere.

He touched it and felt his fingers seep into its surface. He shook, rived by a current, with a square of light appearing in the cortex of his brain and within it a wheeling gyre. He moved back, placing his hands which felt hot underneath his armpits. He was confused and dis-orientated. His mind had sourced a vision whose meaning he could not penetrate. Swinging the lamp wildly about him he searched for a way out.

As he scrambled around the chamber he had the eerie feeling of a substantial presence stalking him at his back. He looked around quickly a number of times only to catch a glimpse of what he thought was an emanation of some kind. The name of Eighad surfaced in his consciousness. For a moment he believed he was re-entering the hallucinogenic world of Bradaz or that the sinister bias of the moun-tain was also integral to this world. Suddenly, within the shadowy light thrown by the lamp he saw Liano standing before him. He recoiled, unsure as to whether she too was a reflection, a medium or some transcendent form. Whichever she was, her anger was evident. Drawing close to him she asked.

'What are you doing here?'

Whether because of the confusion which had rooted itself in his imagination or the very real anger communicated to him, he felt profoundly intimidated. He apologised briefly and said.

'Take me out of here.'

Once in the main vestibule Hadge regained his composure and probed Liano as to the nature of the cavern.

'There are areas which are off limits. Tomorrow I will give you a map. There are dangers inherent in everything. In Aganatz there are extremes. You move from the beaten track at your own risk, as I do.' When he pressed her to give an explanation of the reflected shape of Bradaz she said, 'There are things here whose meaning and signifi-cance is unclear. Not everything is comprehensible to me.'

During the following weeks Hadge occupied his time in exploring the vast terrain of the garden, taking notes and accomplishing a selection of drawings with the use of Eighad's old materials. He was attempting to achieve an overview of the system which underlay it, to fabricate a thesis through the detailing of recurrent patterns. He was also working on the enlargement of some biographical notations and had undertaken a close scrutiny of the remnants of Eighad's notebooks which had been carefully placed at the bottom of his trunk.

The bulk of these notebooks were fragmentary but they communicated the over-riding impression of a violent and abusive man, who over the course of the years he spent with Olan, had been a malicious and manipulative presence, creating an insidious psychological dependency which he continually turned to his advantage. Hadge felt a strong moral antipathy to this man, who had derived pleasure from actively undermining Olan's sense of self in his maniacal subjection of her to his will. In one entry Eighad had outlined an alternating pattern of confirmation and denial regarding the veracity of Olan's statements, questioning the nature of her memory and ultimately relishing the inducement of a profound sense of paranoia.

At different points Olan appeared to have achieved a measure of control over both herself and her situation and in time had become a formidable adversary. Eighad's last entries described a growing boredom and desire to quit Aganatz. He speculated in the course of this entry on perpetrating a final violence on Olan. There was no further elaboration. In the end Hadge was benignly indifferent to what he deduced was the probable murder of Eighad at the hands of Olan. He did not discuss the notebooks with Liano, understanding that her view of Eighad was based on an abstract idealisation, and he was not in the habit of destroying illusions.

Given the time to mull over details of his own past he found himself returning to incidents in his childhood which had remained as unconscious corrugations in his memory, occasional irritants subliminally discharging their venom. The bulk of his investigations related to his mother who had died during a flu epidemic. He was subsequently taken into the care of a local family. In the intervening years he had pieced together his mother's history.

Her name had been Evina, a dancer who had travelled south at an early age and who had worked for a number of troupes on the circuit which stretched from coast to coast. She had been in her late twenties and nearing the end of her career when she conceived Hadge. The father, according to those sources who knew her, had been a painter. Hadge's main source for these recollections was a fellow dancer of Evina's, called Quarat, a statuesque negress whom he had finally located a few weeks prior to his visit to Limbah.

Quarat kept a brothel in Falaheel, a market town on the northern perimeter of the Gulf. Situated near the harbour and the main souk, she specialised in orientals. Each interview he conducted with her had to be paid for in kind with opium. It was a gesture which validated the usurpation of her time. Reclining opulently on an imported divan she related all she knew of Evina and described their relationship.

'Evina was smart. Always looking ahead to the time she'd no longer be able to dance. She taught me a lot.

'We'd all saved some money and I asked her if she wanted to help me set up this house. We were friends. I trusted her. She said she'd think about it.

'During our last winter together we were quartered in Abudan. New sets had been commissioned. Evina became involved with one of the artists. I don't recall his name.

'She was more interested in his craft than anything else and believed if she learned it well enough it would provide her with a livelihood in the years ahead.

'He was a severe man, maybe thirty at the time, kept to himself and wouldn't have anything to do with anyone else except Evina. He taught her to paint but she was gifted anyhow and didn't need him. She never loved him and was indifferent when he finally left, even though she was pregnant with you at the time.

'After she left the troupe I heard from her now and then and knew that she had begun to establish a reputation for herself as a painter in her own right. After she died I thought of taking you in myself but as you can imagine this was hardly the place to bring up a child. You understand.'

Hadge's memories of his time with his mother were vague but they were infused with a warmth and loving attention which vanished when he was taken in by his adoptive parents, a couple whom he had registered as hostile from the beginning. They were introduced to him as Mr and Mrs Said. Hadge consistently felt himself to be the root cause of the tensions which pervaded the household. It was only in later years that this guilt was dissembled.

Maim, the wife, was an asexual creature with a neurotic insistence on cleanliness. She had an aversion to any physical demonstration of affection and insisted that Yeusef go elsewhere for what she openly described as his genital pleasure. The husband, an outwardly mild man was content with the nature of this resolution but over the years he had tampered with Hadge and so wreaked a kind of perverted sexual revenge on his wife, Maim. It was memories of this period which Hadge had carefully submerged in the strata of his sub-conscious and which now and again resurfaced in night terrors and obscure anxieties.

It was this fracturing in his childhood, this emotional disembow-elment which he viewed as the source of his consistent failure to breathe real life and vigour into his relationships. It was these memories which stopped him at a certain point from dedicating himself more totally to those he loved. He realised that he had no loving ideal against which to measure the strength and distinction of any particular involvement. This led him in the main to conduct short term, if intense, affairs.

With Liano he perceived a difference. She was as isolated and as ruptured as he felt himself to be, and perhaps together in this strange landscape he could finally discharge the guilt and hatred still abiding in his memory. Was it not time, he asked himself, to stand firm in one patch of ground and reward himself with the thing which would rehabilitate and align him most fervently with the natural pattern of things? What lay ahead was the opportunity to invest himself with someone, with Liano, who owed nothing to the abberations of his past.

He decided over time to propose to Liano that they begin a family together. For all he knew they had already done so. Their lovemaking had been feverish and rewarding and who was to say that Liano had not already conceived. He was convinced she would agree to this bonding. It was she after all, who had coaxed him to stay, she who shared her love with him so guilelessly and showered herself over him.

Walking down the steps of the tower some days later, Hadge entered into bright sunlight to the vociferous clamour of ubu finches whose intense red breasts stood out from the clustering bunches of hanging dates. He had grown used to these flamboyant and super-abundant aspects of the garden, and while he still viewed them as remarkable they had integrated themselves naturally into the fabric of his consciousness.

He made for the orchard grove at the southern end of the garden where Liano had told him she would be until late morning. He caught sight of her when he was half way through the great marrow planta-tion whose outlandish tubers spawned on top of raised beds of ochre-tinged clay. He stood for a moment in almost voyeuristic acclamation of this woman whom he had seen change quite radically during the course of the last months. Standing in a white robe linearly striped with thin red lines, she was bagging the massive blago fruits which were reminiscent of giant apples. Her now formidably lobed breasts caused the fabric to pleat in the centre when she bent to pick some fruit off the ground. Calling to her, he saw her rise, smile, and then place her hands in a relaxed fashion on her hips.

Embracing, they stood for a while in silence, melting the buffer of their short absence from each other. When they sat down Hadge went through a process of reconfirming for himself his appeal for her, her appeal for him, and a more general mental validation of the course of action he had in mind. It pointed to his own insecurities that he should question her love for him. In the ultimate formulation of his desire, he said,

'Liano, I've been here for over three months now. Everything here stimulates me to stay. I feel more dedicated, both to you and this place, than I have felt to anyone or anything, for a very long time. Do you understand?'

Liano nodded.

'I want the walls and trees to bear witness to me now when I tell you that I want you and love you, and that this is the simplest and most profound articulation of my feelings I have ever made to anyone, and that I will abide with you always.'

He stopped. There were tears in both their eyes. He had said nothing of children but he knew Liano understood, somehow it was implicit, and that this too would come in time. Liano held him close, tears now streaming from her eyes. She cried voluptuously and thought her heart would burst with emotion.

So began a period of loving exploration, a time when they felt all things sufficient to their needs, and they themselves a perfect complement of souls. For Liano it was the exuberant fulfilment of the hopes she had harboured when she first rescued Hadge. Eight weeks after Hadge's heartfelt dedication of himself Liano announced she was pregnant.

After the initial shock and realisation that things were falling into place more quickly than he had expected, Hadge expressed his great joy and decided with Liano's approval to move to a new part of the Fortress, knowing that the stairs of the north tower would eventually prove too much for her.

His feelings at this time had a complex orientation. The baby, or the idea of the baby, ramified his existence in some way, forwarding his life compulsively. He understood the change in terms of a new and pivotal insight, one which refreshed his senses and caused an abandonment of old precepts, recharging a jaded mind. It was a new focus and because of it he felt more deliberately human. It was an ancestral linking, a connectedness which secured him powerfully to the world.

Isolating a few rooms out of all the empty space in the Fortress proved to be a difficult task. Objections were raised as to the quality of light, proximity to certain sections of the garden, level of noise and so on. Finally it was decided that some ground floor apartments in the southern wing should be renovated as quickly as possible. To accomplish this in time for the birth Hadge suspended work on his own writings. After initial misgivings as to the choice, he gradually grew to like its southern aspect and the fact that it looked out onto one of the few broad clearances of grassland.

During the first months of her pregnancy Liano worked industriously by his side, cleaning walls, stripping floors, occasionally uncovering details of previous occupants, delicate ornamental work which Hadge was inclined to preserve but which Liano insisted be obliterated. Hadge deferred. She had a particular aesthetic which she wished to impose on these rooms, one which Hadge did not try to ameliorate since he knew that he could set up his own quarters according to his own taste in some other part of the Fortress. When it came to furniture Hadge began to wander aimlessly around the various wings looking to cull oddments from different rooms. He also began to make some new pieces from hardwoods which had fallen down over the years.

His intimacy with both the Fortress and the garden grew as a result of these labours.

The Fortress he now believed to be a calendraic unit of extraordinary sophistication incorporating a variety of geometric forms. He had already verified its alignment in relation to the spring equinox. The building as a whole seemed rendered in such a way as to chart the sun's movements, and its architectural justifications were not random. The more Hadge discovered, the more he realised the fluency of the system. In a more abstract fashion than with the mirroring accretion of the rock of Bradaz, Aganatz appeared to his mind as an axis of reflection. He was prepared to concede that making assumptions on such a scale was perhaps extravagant, but he sensed that the builders of Aganatz had long ago accessed and incorporated a universal axiom or truth and that the structure had become a point of reflexive integration of the celestial system. To some extent this appeared to be borne out in the garden whose pathways and irrigation channels he charted roughly. Working backwards and forwards

from the centre point of the lake, which he believed to be both the real
and symbolic representation of the source of life, he discovered the
ancient Sanskrit word for God repeated over and over. All in all it
seemed like an archaic and irreducible system which he had barely
glimpsed and whose ultimate breakdown was unknowable.

The garden had become for him a domain of animal and vegetal
struggles and transgressions. Primary among these was the disease
he had first noticed by the lake some months back. He thought it had
vanished or lingered on in a minor way but now he realised that it
had entered a remote part of the garden, one which was virtually
inaccessible, and had in a few short weeks killed the bulk of the plants
or reduced once thriving trees to one or two sprigs of life. The whole
chain of life in this north eastern section had been affected with the
smell of rotting carcasses becoming so intense in the midday heat that
Hadge bypassed the area altogether or wore a muslin mask for
protection. Some of the larger animals which had been comfortably
contained within this area now began to range over new terrain in
search of food. Liano remained unperturbed. She had seen worse
occur within the confines of the Fortress and was convinced that this
minor incident would right itself in time. To Hadge the affected area
represented a destabilisation in the equilibrium of the garden. It
worried him and he began to think of ways of treating it. The density
of rotting matter had created a volatile situation, literally a combus-
tible aroma hung in the air. After watching it for eight days Hadge
concluded that the disease had a moody range. There were days of
recession when flowerings and plant regenerations occurred, when
the animals were active and communicated the sense of their being
incorporated within the folds and strata of a well balanced predatory
system. This could change overnight and would be preluded by
horrific screams which sounded like creatures in the throes of slow
strangulation.

After a period of days, when the spread of the disease appeared to
have stemmed itself, Hadge relaxed his guard and returned to what
Liano insisted ought to be his primary concern, that of preparing a

habitable abode for the baby to be. Liano told him of a set of chairs she wanted and which, as she remembered it, were in one of the upper rooms on the third floor.

'If they haven't been eaten by termites,' she said, 'they'd be ideal for the main room. See if you can find them.'

With a map furnished by Liano he went in search of them. It took him two hours to locate the room which he then found to be locked. He pushed sturdily against the old door until finally it gave way opening into semi-darkness. What appeared to be heavy velour drapes fell in moth-eaten columnar folds down to the floor. A heavy sideboard with gilded silver stood against the long wall to the left while the four handsome high-backed chairs were arranged with some formality around a marble fireplace. Hadge felt himself to be standing among the remnants of a clichéd drawingroom setting, with the air of an antique civility still discreetly fragrant. Lighting the lamp which he carried with him he began to walk across the room towards the window. His feet shifted slightly with each step and he heard a series of grinding crunches. He suspected a littering of cockroaches or some other insect. Such had occurred in other derelict rooms he had inadvertently entered. Moving the lamp below his waist, he realised it was not a carpet of polished roachwings which glinted back, but a floor covered inches deep in teeth. He bent down to pick up a handful and these he took outside into the light of the corridor. They were human teeth. There was no doubt in his mind. Thinking that this random sample was unusual he returned, retrieved a larger number and examined them. These too were human teeth, some of children others of adults. There were any number of sinister scenarios to explain their presence but Hadge ultimately reckoned on their being part of a burial ritual in some previous era. This didn't explain however why they were in an otherwise ornately furnished room. Throwing the handful of teeth back into the room he closed the door and began to make his way down the corridor. The more he tried to evolve antidotal explanations for what he had found, the more threatened he became. Violent images seemed to conjure themselves out of air and heavy shadows to take on a gruesome animate charge. It was in this atmosphere of disorientation that he took a wrong turning from the one indicated on the map. Although he realised his mistake quickly his efforts to retrace his steps compounded his initial lapse of concentration. He could feel his own fear. His palms were clammy, a small vein by his right temple throbbed. He walked in this uncharted territory for what seemed like hours. Darkness was beginning to fall and his lamp's store of oil to dwindle when he caught sight of a figure slipping round a distant corner. When he reached the end of the corridor the figure was ahead of him. It was a woman. She was naked and from the rear he thought for a moment that it was Liano, then he realised it was not. She moved slowly, the sides of her shimmering buttocks lolling from side to side. She had a ghostly transparency as though she was a memoried form whose projected image was at one point concentrated and substantial and at the next tenuous and flimsy. She stopped, turned sideways and entered through a door. Her belly, obscured up to then, showed she was pregnant. Hadge wanted to turn back but he could not, his feet moved him forward until he stood facing in on the room.

He had no idea where the light was coming from but every detail inside was visible. The room was completely red. Every crevice and pore sweated the colour, every splinter of wood protruded like a bloodied thorn. The only article of furniture was a table, placed to the left. This had been painted black. On top of it reposed the heavy bones of a large skeleton.

Hadge watched as the woman went over to the table, clasped an upper rib in her fist and broke it off. Taking the rib she cut into her flesh and drew a bloody circle around her huge belly. In nightmarish progression her womb fell out, leaving a developed foetus in a membraneous skin to squirm on the floor. Hadge could take no more and went instinctively to gather the child up, but he could not move past the threshold of the door. When he looked at the woman again her stomach was sealed and flat. Taking the gasping foetus by the legs she brought it to the skeleton whose neck vertebrae appeared to flex making the head jerk upwards. The skeletal jaws opened and the woman fed the child in, head first. The woman turned to Hadge as she did this, a bloodcurdling smile widening her lips, her toothless gums gashed and bleeding. The door closed automatically in his face and he ran. He ran until he could run no further. When he stopped he saw the light of the main vestibule usher him to safety. He fell to his knees and called, screamed for Liano, but she was nowhere in sight.

—   ~   —

As Liano's pregnancy progressed Hadge grew accustomed to her food fetishes, her occasional binges and to a level of emotionalism which he had neither predicted nor prepared himself for. Liano became for him a human territory of ill-resolved feelings. No amount of cherishing or loving seemed to solace her sufficiently, or provide her with the store of trust she needed to lessen the turbulence of her moods.

Initially she had experienced days of exhaustion when the sheer effort of hauling her sluggish body from bed was too much for her. Then would come periods when her whole system was adrenalated and aggressive, and under the pretext of the apartment not being finished she would berate Hadge endlessly, to the point where arguments ensued. Hadge tried to understand, tried to condition his responses and compromise his feelings but often he found himself reflecting her state of alienation and detachment. He worried about the child when Liano clattered about in a condition of frenzy and wondered whether or not she was trying to lose it.

In his efforts to rationalise her feelings he saw her responses as being natural. Here after all was a life burgeoning within her, a capsulated existence feeding on her reserves, a centre capsizing her spirit inwards. Her broodiness, even her bovine aspect was surely an inescapable internalisation, a necessary distortion of her system, a

reflective absorption and identification with the child, making outside challenges in her life and most particularly her relationship to
Hadge, difficult, and of secondary importance.

With this in mind he provided her with tangible evidence of his
love. He was deferential, contrite, adoring, encouraging. Some of
these efforts seemed to restore her humour but in the main she grew
more taciturn and distant as the pregnancy advanced.

After seven months Liano's belly was well distended and the
apartments almost complete. It was around this time that Liano
approached Hadge with the rib of her father. She requested that he
take her to his grave. Hadge had never disclosed to Liano what he
had witnessed that night in the upper reaches of the southern wing,
but the sight of the rib in her hand recalled the intensity and horror
of the vision. Taking the rib from her as though it was a knife, he said,

'Why do you want to see it now? Why not wait until after the birth?
The journey will be too hazardous for you in this heat.'

'No. The time is now. Hadge, I can't explain why exactly, put it
down to my mood or perhaps a need to bear witness to the place
where he died, before the baby's born. I don't know.'

Hadge agreed, but only on the provision that they take three days
to accomplish the journey, so as not to place undue stress on her
system. The plan was to set out two days later.

Hadge's apprehension about going just then was related not only
to Liano but also to the garden. The disease had not abated but had
spread insidiously and now threatened areas in the west and east
roughly half the size of the garden. He believed that it was only
through his application of a lime sulphur treatment that the rest of
the garden was still intact. The thought of leaving the Fortress at such
a crucial stage was against his better judgement. Had he not considered Liano's request as an emotional plea, a deep-seated desire to
invest herself with her past and prayerfully commune with her
father's spirit, he would not have relented. But it was the kind of
appeal he understood and it was with this reckoning of its importance
to her that he set about gathering provisions for their departure.

With their preparations complete, Hadge and Liano set out at daybreak. It was a mild morning with a light wind blowing easterly across the desert. Liano was in better form and wore one of her mother's old garments, a loose, flowing green robe flecked with yellow. Hadge responded to her good humour and began to feel less apprehensive about the journey ahead, however he could not but recollect his harrowing experiences in the desert now almost a year past.

After the sun had risen the wind diminished. Hadge protected Liano from the most intense rays with a large multi-coloured parasol with gold tassels hanging from its rim. Once they had ascended the main ridge two miles north of the Fortress, the great mountain of Bradaz came firmly into view. From this distance and perspective it appeared even larger than when he had approached it from Limbah.

After passing a braid of dunes on the far side of the ridge Hadge staked the long pole parasol and settled down to rest and eat a little. He looked at Liano under the slanting shade shrouding her upper body. As he did so he had to suppress an instantaneous feeling of nausea. Whether it was because of the quality of the light or the peculiar coloration of her robe he could not be certain, but at that moment Liano exuded the horrific appearance and demeanour of a large lizard. As he tried to rid his mind of the image Liano turned her face towards him, a face suddenly knarled and lumpish with a lizard-like tongue slipping out over her lower lip. Responding to his obvious state of alarm she asked him if anything was the matter. In an effort to regain his composure he muttered a meaningless *non sequitur*, walked quickly over a low dune to his right and in a pretence of urination collected himself.

He reasoned that it was the nightmarish reality of his past which had conjured the image and that it would take a conscious effort on his part to withstand such subconscious intrusions in the days that lay ahead. Although still visibly shaken he returned to Liano who was now sitting on her bottom, her face tranquil and restored. Offering his hand he drew her up and in a forced gesture, kissed her on the lips.

By late afternoon they had reached the first of the steep ravines which lay at the base of Bradaz. In a sheltered stone well, they stopped and rested for a while. Both were absorbed by different concerns and when they shattered the silence it was in an effort to bridge the gap between them. Looking at the map Liano suggested they spend the night in the cave.

'We should be able to make the grave by midday tomorrow if we cut diagonally north,' said Liano.

Hadge had hoped to avoid the cave altogether but with the sun declining fast he realised they had little choice.

'Have you considered the possibility, Liano, that we won't be able to find the grave? There were no boulders in the vicinity to act as markers and these map coordinates are approximate. With so small an area it may prove difficult.'

'Is there any reason you don't want me to find it?'

'No, of course not. I'm just saying it's a possibility. Remember it was mere coincidence that I came upon it in the first place. Who's to say I'll be able to find it again.'

'Well I don't have any such doubts. And there's no use trying to hide it any longer. I know you were against this expedition in the first place. If you want to turn back now it's fine by me. I'll go on alone.'

'No.'

Hadge began to pack up their belongings. Urging Liano to hurry he began to climb upwards towards the mouth of the cave. Stopping frequently Hadge tried to shake off his misgivings about the trip and to focus his mind and energies on the task of finding the grave. There was a chance his own dig would have left a depression or that some of the bones would have impeded the sand in a particular way.

It was dusk when they reached the clearing in front of the cave and with some twigs and wood pieces he had brought with him from Aganatz, Hadge set about building a fire. In the last hour of their climb the desert had begun to cool rapidly and as Liano sat on a large boulder Hadge advised her to wrap up with another wool jacket and keep warm.

Only a few months previously this affectionate concern would have met with a gentle rebuke as to his worrisome nature, but now in the flickering light thrown by the fire all he could see was a scowl disfiguring her face. Hadge tried to locate in his mind the cause of this change, this disgruntlement. He remembered something Liano had said during the early part of the pregnancy.

'I don't want this baby to be the only thing between us. There must be more. Do you really love me aside from it?'

He had assured her he did but the feeling persisted that the depth of their bond related directly to the child. Was it not true that he was most profoundly in love with the idea of the child, with its possibility, its newness, and when set against a rancorous and emotional woman didn't it seem a much easier thing to love? No, he told himself. He loved her in terms of her own human possibilities. The child was a connection, a part of the bond, what he loved would remain with her, and after the baby was born, they would grow close together again.

He watched as Liano lay down on her back, bundled beneath a heavy blanket. The night was full of stars and as he looked towards them his mind turned to the garden. He was worried. He believed that their survival depended on that of the garden. This was an illogical identification since he knew that there were more than enough supplies and stores to see them through many years. Long enough certainly to revive the garden should it succumb. Still something inside him said that the garden should not be allowed to perish.

Hadge bedded down beside Liano, pulling the large felt coverlet over his shoulders. He had thought, before setting out, that sleep in this place of memories would be difficult and as he lay listening to Liano's sleeping wheeze he breathed deeply in an effort to relax himself. As the night grew colder his heart beat increased and he could not rid himself of the idea that the cave was bursting at the seams with spirits stacked from floor to roof behind his head. He tried to turn his head but fear locked his neck. Liano seemed to be part of it. When she moved in her sleep and accidentally brushed against his flesh he saw her as a corrupt organism, with worms and maggots

wriggling from her pores, trying to gain a foothold on his skin. Shortly
before daybreak he fell asleep and it seemed only minutes later when
he was being roused.

Feeling exhausted he chewed on some bethel leaves and drank
some tea Liano had prepared. He began to feel better. When they had
their things packed Hadge told Liano that he wanted to take a quick
look inside the cave before departing. It was not indolent curiosity
which prompted him to do this but a desire to confront the fear which
had racked him during the night. With a small lamp he moved inside.
At first there was nothing, no sinister presences, nothing to indicate
the existence of a presiding malevolence. As he moved deeper, the air
became cloying, the walls tepid to the touch and laying his head closer
to the ground he heard a faint churning sound. Swinging the lamp
low he came to the edge of a sewer-like cavity from which issued the
noxious smells of molten rock. Bradaz, he realised to his horror, was
active. He thought immediately of Liano.

Walking quickly to the mouth of the cave he almost shouted at her.

'Liano, let's get out of here now.'

'Why? What's the matter?'

'Bradaz is active. I could smell the lava back there. For all I know
it's about to go up.'

'Don't be ridiculous. As far ...'

He didn't allow her to finish.

'Listen I'm not prepared to argue. Let's just go.'

Walking steadily down the northern slope it took them half an hour
to clear the final outlying boulders, with Hadge looking back continually, checking to see whether the cone was smoking. Liano called out
to him to slow down.

'Bradaz,' she said, 'hasn't been active for centuries.'

'How do you know?'

'Mother told me. Ask any traveller on the southern routes and he'll
tell you the same.'

'Well there's something stirring in its bowels now, and the sooner
we get out of here the better.'

With Bradaz behind them, Hadge began to consult the map at regular intervals and with the aid of the compass he adhered as closely as possible to the plotted course.

Finally they stopped at a point where the dense gravel gave way to a finer grade on a very gentle slope leading down to a broad hollow. Without looking at the map Hadge felt sure that this was the place. For what it was worth, their compass readings seemed to concur. However, it was only now when they had agreed upon a spot that they realised the extent of their difficulties. Removing his sandals Hadge began to walk a broad area in a roughly systematic manner. Holding the rib in front of her like a diviner Liano tried to find the generating quiver of her father's bones. She stopped at different points and pawed the shifting layers of sand without success. From some distance away Hadge could hear her mumbling to herself. Fearing that the whole exercise might prove too stressful, he began to walk towards her in the hope of persuading her to make a prayerful act and leave.

Before he reached her she had gone to the pack to retrieve the shovel Hadge had brought with him.

'No Liano,' he called. 'Leave that to me.'

'He's here somewhere,' she said. Her voice was like a little girl's.

Taking the shovel from her, he began to dig. Throughout the course of the afternoon he threw up mounds of sand like some perplexed hound. It was pointless, he knew that, but the effort had to be made. By sunset he was exhausted, and going to her, he tried to help her to articulate her sense of loss, but it only made him feel inadequate, superfluous. He left her with her long suppressed grief and hoped that the pain she was feeling would at some point inform her in a positive way. For hours into the night she sat amongst the anthill swarm of dunes, sobbing, the tip of Eighad's rib between her hands, abstractedly patterning a surface layer of sand. It was only after having exhausted herself through tears that she finally lay down and slept.

What good had it done, he asked himself, stirring up these old memories? He looked at Liano and felt only pity. He felt removed from her in this watershed of her pain and thought of his mother and of his own sense of loss, in an attempt to stimulate an empathetic condition of remorse.

They left at daybreak with Hadge telling her to take a few minutes to make her peace with whatever presences lay beneath the ground.

On the homeward trek they made good time, bypassing Bradaz altogether. Looking at it from a distance Hadge imagined it as a livid thing, wavering in the midday heat. He felt relieved that the journey was almost over. Did it matter that the cache of bones was again subsumed and irretrievable? Was that not as it should be? At least she still had the rib as relic of his life, a physical symbol which would solace her.

Without having to follow the route of the map, they were able to head directly south and by early afternoon they had reached the final ridge leading to Aganatz. Standing on the narrow plateau, Hadge found himself surprised that it still existed. The intensity of the sun made it appear almost white with its walls visibly stimulated, expressing an animate charge. He could hear Liano's footsteps on the shale bed a short distance behind him. As he continued to look at the Fortress his first image of it returned to him. In his mind's eye he lifted his head from the pallet board, his neck muscles taut and sinewy. Again he saw something move on the battlements. He tried to focus more accurately and was sure that the shape represented a figure. Each time he had recalled the memory he had sensed that something was missing, some memoried detail had remained buried. Now he recognised the missing factor in that long recorded memory as a figure and the reality of its presence on that day had the insistence of a truth. Not a figment, not an hallucination. Someone had been there. He could not say what led him to be persuaded of this as a fact but he was certain now, as in a way he had been during the first weeks of his discovery, that Liano was not alone in the Fortress.

When Liano came and stood by his side he looked at her in a new light. What amount of contained secrets remained between them? He did not feel he could broach her with a direct question, so he said nothing. His thoughts took on a subversive complexity. Mentally he began to describe and interrogate her various actions trying to find a pattern which would indicate her having had contact with someone else. If someone else did exist, then why this insistence on secrecy? His only course, he believed, was to follow her movements over the following days. To attempt a systematic search of the Fortress was, despite his understanding of the principles upon which it was founded, tantamount to madness.

Within half a mile of the Fortress the winds which had turned south south west carried a putrid stench from the direction of the garden. Something had occurred in their absence. Both were worried, but for different reasons.

Liano, although she found it difficult to think about her mother, suspected that Olan had somehow freed herself and wreaked some havoc within the temple of the walls. Forced to think about this possibility Liano had also to confront the fact of her neglect. In the course of her relationship with Hadge, Olan had figured merely as a hindrance, as an obstacle to the exploration of her developing passion for Hadge. Liano believed that her mother, through her insidious questions, insinuations and pleas, would somehow divert and malign her love, her ambition, and the range of her possible fulfilment with him. She feared her mother's ability to make her feel guilty and it was this threat more than any other which made her initially disinclined to spend time catering to Olan's needs. During the first months of Hadge's recovery Liano had seen fit to provide her with food and water on a regular basis but the scrupulousness of her attention had waned. On her last visit, a month previously, the stench emanating from her mother's quarters had been almost unbearable. She had filled the side unit with stores, replaced it against the main frame and left. She could not bear to look at Olan and wore a mask over face within the airless confines of the room. She knew her mother was dying but felt incapable of addressing the fact. Now the thought of Hadge seeing this version of her mother loose in the garden frightened her. Nearing the gates she wanted to suggest that she go in alone, but she could not formulate a reason for such an action without making him suspicious.

By the time they reached the gates of Aganatz the overwhelming stench had forced them to mask their faces. They left their supplies beyond the walls in the belief that they might have to spend some time outside of the Fortress.

On opening the great gates all they could see was a thick vapourish mist rising up from different sections of the garden. The birds and animals were in an uproar and it sounded as though large numbers of them had grouped into a herd and were stampeding *en masse* towards the open spaces along the western perimeter. Because the volume of steam rising from the earth occluded all but a vague outline of the most prominent trees, it was difficult to discern what kind of condition the garden was actually in. Hadge suspected the worst and believed that the disease had taken a firm hold. Liano tugged on his robe and they moved slowly in the direction of the north tower.

Standing in Eighad's old room they spoke of their options. Hadge knew what she was going to suggest.

'We've no choice but to burn it to the ground.'

'The southern part,' said Hadge, 'is probably still unaffected. If we could use the water wheel to fill the main channels which strike through the centre then maybe we could contain a fire begun among the northern groves. There's no point in over-reacting and destroying something which we could alter over time.'

They agreed that they should begin at sunrise the following morning.

That night Hadge remained in the tower while Liano went to her old room on the pretext of retrieving some fresh clothes. After watching the flare of her light fade, Hadge left the tower and followed her movements. She stopped first at one of the storerooms to the left of the kitchen, on the ground floor of the southern wing. Into a small wooden cart she placed a selection of jars and preserves together with compacted blocks of dried fruit. Although the cries and barks of animals were still audible, the clamour had diminished substantially as had the offensive stench which earlier had been so oppressive. Whether this was a change conjunctive with darkness or the first hint of a dramatic re-stabilisation, he did not know. He was absorbed by these thoughts when he saw Liano move off in the direction of the main vestibule. Walking steadily with the cart trailing behind her she entered the parallel corridor system to the left of the main entrance. He realised at this point that if she intended ascending to the upper stories with the cart she would have to use the ramp system, a complex pattern of slopes and inclines integrated into the outer wall of each wing. It was a system he had always shied away from because of their inaccessibility and tendency to move sideways and occasionally downward, leading inevitably to a state of confusion.

The route she took was strange even by the standards of the Fortress with her lamp illuminating garishly-painted corridors from the walls of which clusters of skulls had been grooved into the heavy masonry. To the rear of the second storey, metres of narrow glass casings stretched on either side of the wall. They were teeming with a variety of scaled and hardbacked insects, grotesque and ancient precursors with twitching antennae and ponderously slow movements. Some cases were on the point of bursting while others were broken and virtually empty. In the vague light afforded by Liano's distant lamp Hadge heard things crunch and squirm beneath his feet.

After passing through a hive of narrow rooms Hadge again smelt the rank odour of the garden and wondered whether or not he had begun to descend. Liano stopped meanwhile and tied a band of cloth around her mouth and nose. The stench was almost unbearable. Liano then entered the anteroom to a larger chamber. Returning to the cart she dragged it into the main room. To the left of the door was a small alcove. Hadge made for it, believing that it would conceal him from view yet allow him occasional glimpses of what Liano was up to. Hunkering down he moved slowly to the side of the corridor. From under the shadowed alcove he secured his first view of the chamber.

PART IV

In the centre of the chamber was a large cage with a tunnel and an enclosed structure to the left. Clipped onto the right side of the massive main frame was a smaller cage. The floor was littered with broken glass, food deposits and what appeared to be a sludge of human waste and other debris. Two sides of the main cage had been thickened with applications of excreta leaving only the front section with the original bars still visible. The mass of garbage on the floor had to be waded through and, as Hadge watched Liano, he saw the mulch rise half way up her calves. At first he could see no human presence within the cage but as he peered closer he began to discern a shape in the far right-hand corner. It was dark brown in colour and broadly ovular in shape. There was a cavity near the top and as it moved slightly he saw another further down. It was through this slight movement that he also spotted the muddied form of an arm and the more clarified contours of a hand. He realised then that locked within this shell of compacted urine and shit was a human form and that it was alive.

Liano was busy filling the smaller cage with the supplies she had brought with her, allowing Hadge to continue to stare at the shape. As he did so he witnessed the manoeuvre by which the shell had been made. A small bowel movement was pushed out through the lower hole, collected carefully by the hand and applied in a thick layer around the base of the shell. Hadge felt intensely nauseated, more by the fact of the shell-bound individual's human disintegration than by the outwardly distressing nature of its retreat towards death. What disturbed him most deeply, however, was Liano's apparent indifference and the casual way in which she went about her duties. He breathed deeply and forced himself to bear witness, if only in an effort to understand the ramifications of the scene or gauge the currents of fear or hatred which existed.

After Liano had filled the smaller of the two cages with food and snapped it back into place she cleared the water sluice which extended from an elevated wooden barrel and then she left. Hadge was faced with the decision as to whether to follow her or remain behind. He had no idea if he could find his way back alone but as he considered his options he realised he had no choice but to attempt to aid the demented creature in the cage. He relaxed a little as he watched Liano vanish into a labyrinth of corridors.

The whole area was now plunged into darkness with only a little moonlight filtering in through a window in an adjoining room. Hadge lit the small lamp he carried with him, stepped out of the alcove and under the lintel of the door. The sludge which filled the room extended into the corridor and he could hear his feet squelch and his soles moisten. He was unsure of what approach to take but as he moved closer he sensed the form register his presence. A slight movement of the hand seemed to betray its anxiety. In an effort to counteract this Hadge began to talk, investing his voice with a concerned distress, making it clear that he meant no harm. He repeated the same phrase over and over.

'I've not come to harm you. Trust me.'

He began to describe his actions. He explained who he was and how he had come to find her.

'Move your hand if you want me to come into the cage and help you.'

For a while there was nothing, then very slowly the hand raised and folded back in a gesture that said, *come.*

Hadge studied the structure of the cage quickly trying to see how the grids could be loosened. Some of the clasps had been encrusted over. These he cleared and making as little noise as possible, he lowered the front grid section. Climbing into the cage he remained in one corner and continued to talk, working out a system of yes and no answers to be indicated by the hand. The questions were unimportant. All he wanted to establish was a level of communication and trust before he moved any closer. The one piece of information he did elicit was that the form locked within this foul shell was Liano's mother, Olan. He tried to concentrate on helping her rather than ponder the implications of this fact.

'Do you want me to remove the shell?'

The answer came. 'Yes.'

Hadge inched closer until he was beside the arm. He took it very gently, felt it shake with fear, pressed it reassuringly between his palms and voiced a comforting platitude.

He thought he could hear sobs through the mouth hole at the top of the shell and such was the level of emotion between them that he had to stem his own tears.

Beginning at the top of the free arm where the crust was thinnest he worked slowly towards the head. The process reminded him of times when, as a child, he had picked the dry flaking scabs from wounds. The skin beneath the shell was parched and wrinkled, the pigment blotched with large red areas and small boils.

The process was slow and painful, especially as he neared the neck where the waste had bonded with body hair and had to be moistened with water to loosen it. The line of the jaw and then the face began to take shape. The features were crinkled, wizened, and the skin's epidermal layers were in a state of decomposition. The eyes remained closed and Hadge did not dare to touch them knowing that it would be days before they should be allowed to register sunlight. Once the face was cleared and cleansed, the rest of her body followed rapidly with large pieces coming away in chunks. The body was nude and displayed the same serious level of decay throughout. It was dawn before the process was complete and as Hadge turned his head away from Olan for a moment he could see some rays of light fan onto the stone slab floor of the adjoining anteroom. There was a sense of terrible, painful relief mixed with confusion. What was he to do next?

Olan had said nothing, could say nothing and was in a desperately frail condition. The first thing to do was to get her out of the chamber. After explaining his intentions, he lifted her gently into his arms and, measuring his steps he walked down the long corridor. In one of the side rooms was a small bed. Having laid her on this he returned to the chamber and filled a pitcher with water. After bathing her thoroughly he wrapped her in a blanket and covered her eyes with a band of soft cloth. Once again he drew her up into his arms and began to trek through the bewildering maze of corridors. At different times during the hours that followed, he had the unusual sense that Olan was aiding him in the decisions he made. It was as though she was guiding his steps, telling him to suspend trust in his own rationale and allow her knowledge of the Fortress to deliver them down safely.

It was nearing midday when they finally descended to the ground floor and Hadge saw the bright expanse of grass extend in front of the southern wing. The mist which had hung over the garden was gone and the plants, even at this distance, seemed to glisten with a recuperative energy. Hadge knew that Liano would have noted his absence and would be searching the grounds and wings of the Fortress in an effort to find him. He was unsure what her reaction would be should she see him with Olan. It was a situation he wanted to avoid. Initially at least, it would be best to hide Olan in a place beyond the normal range of Liano's movements. He did not want Olan in the vicinity when he finally confronted Liano.

There was a furnished room in the east wing which he had come upon by chance some months previously, one which he had thought of converting to a study when time allowed and which Liano did not seem to know about. For the moment the important thing was to keep Olan's presence a secret from Liano, at least temporarily. He had no interest in promoting the same kind of deception Liano had indulged in. Only more evil and bitterness would be engendered by such manoeuvres.

After making sure Olan's eye band was secure, he walked out into the rich sunlight keeping close to the plantation of trees which fringed the perimeter of the plain. Proximity to the trees and shrubs provoked a response from Olan. She stirred in his arms and the pallor of her skin appeared to change. Animal life seemed responsive to her on some level and, as Hadge carried her through a grove of olive trees flocks of birds chorused in apparent recognition of her return. Hadge was afraid this sudden commotion would alert Liano and so he moved more quickly, cutting through the orchard groves which opened onto one of the narrow gravel paths which led to the most easterly of the two main entrances.

The east wing was the most flamboyant of the four and still possessed the antique features of an opulent and expressive period. The room in which he ensconced her had two long windows hung with faded green velour drapes and looked out onto the garden. A large four-poster bed was settled against the centre of one wall with an ornate writing table pushed in against the far corner. On the marble mantelpiece surround were two free-form turquoise pots and some ornaments of oriental origin. The room hinted at clutter yet was spare in the actual number of artifacts it contained. Some weeds and other plants had, over time, begun to colonise gaps in the stone flooring. After placing Olan on the bed, Hadge explained his course of action to her and went in search of Liano.

Now that he turned his attention to Liano, he tried to articulate what his feelings were towards her. He did not understand her actions, did not condone them, but neither could he induce a judgemental fervour. He felt distanced from her, alienated in a way, perhaps because he had never suspected her capable of such a deed. It was this failure to intuit her dark side which made him feel both vulnerable and lacking in a crucial way. He faulted himself, believing that he had been too self-obsessed, too unresponsive. Had he been less so then perhaps she would have trusted him enough to communicate the nature of her dilemma.

After a furious search he found her where he least expected. Returning to the south wing he passed through the kitchens and into the renovated area of their new apartments. Hearing a shuffling noise in the vicinity of the bedroom he went to investigate. There he found Liano scrunched up into one corner, her head buried between her knees. She was rocking back and forth. As he knelt down beside her he could see her eyes were glazed. Her mumbling was mantra-like in its rhythm. She repeated the same phrase,

'I'm going to die. I'm going to die.'

Hadge spoke to her gently, trying to reassure her, but she refused to be pulled from the fixed world of her incanted fear. Her eyes were impenetrable and she shuffled warily beyond his reach when he tried to touch her.

Hadge was certain that she had seen him with Olan and that this was the reason for her terror, her retreat. She was afraid of death. But who, he asked himself, was going to kill her? He broached the subject cautiously and spoke to her as he would a child.

'Liano,' he said. 'Olan is safe. She will recover in time. What you did was wrong but there is no reason to be afraid. I am not angry with you. In time Olan, too, will come to forgive you.'

The words hung in the air as though they had been spoken for his benefit not hers. They had not been communicated and they disintegrated in the void which existed between them.

Hadge remained with her until dusk trying to placate her, to cajole her back to a rational perspective and help her to disclose and confront her fears. He worried about the baby. Was this level of trauma going to affect the child? Should he return to Olan? He decided he fulfilled a greater need by remaining with Liano. Besides, there was little he could do for Olan at this point. What she needed most was rest. As darkness fell Hadge lit a lamp in the bedroom and went to prepare some food. When he returned, the rhythm of Liano's words, which had subsided to a low hum, increased again. He screamed at her,

'Stop it, Liano. Stop it.'

This only induced a new level of panic, making her pack herself more tightly into the corner. Her breathing was erratic and Hadge watched as her distended stomach heaved up and down. He settled himself on the corner of the bed once more but said nothing. He believed that his unthreatening presence would eventually reassure her sufficiently so that she could draw herself beyond the distortions of her imagined world and return to a level of normality.

When he awoke early the following morning his mind was free of the preoccupations which had filled his head the previous day. For a moment he simply relished the heat of the sun filtering through the large shuttered window. He was vaguely anticipatory and even thought briefly of what he had to accomplish in the garden that day. His body felt relaxed. As a backdrop to these sensations he heard a noise from some part of the room. The word 'die' filled the room and sitting up in the bed he looked over at Liano.

She looked drawn and tired. He wondered if she had slept at all. The food which he had left by her side remained untouched. She had not stirred from the corner and her muscles were rigid with tension. Her mantra now sounded like a circular weave of words, her only solace. Hadge thought of it now as a kind of mental conditioning, a protection of sorts. He tried to talk to her but it was useless. She remained locked into her rhythm as though to let go of it would shatter each cell in her body, like glass.

Hadge left some fresh food by her side and went to check on Olan.

As he walked through the garden he witnessed an intense level of activity. The trees and flowers had taken on a new aura. There was a radiant, almost fulminant light generated. Something urged him to move under the swelling canopy which fanned out from the central area, in and around the lake. During the time he had remained at Aganatz he had come to view this watery centre as a mystical arena. He sensed it as the locus of the garden, a riotous and uncharted section which he approached warily. Once within this vault of greenery, the prospect of finding himself isolated intimidated him. Most of the paths which weaved through the rest of the garden became impassable within the echo zone of the great noria wheel.

As he moved towards the lake the gravel pathway he had taken melted gradually into a dense ground level tracery of vines and creepers. A trampled animal track led off to his left and, following this, he located one of the wide irrigation channels which ran in spoke-like formation out from the centre of the garden. He heard the rustle of animals in the vicinity and, standing behind a great cypress, caught sight of a herd of large boars. They were agitated. Hadge stepped back slowly, his eyes searching the lower branch system in case they charged and he had to make good his escape. Suddenly, as though some organising sound had seared its way into their brains, they moved off *en masse* towards the lake, their squeals rising above the noise of stampeding hooves. Hadge breathed deeply and walked steadily towards a plantation of bamboo about half a mile from the western fringe of the lake.

He was surprised to find that evidence of the disease was now limited to odd leaves rather than whole trees or shrubs. The yellow splotching where it did exist was less intense. Once again he began to experience an alternative atmosphere in the garden as a whole. Gone was the sense of an organic structure held in a state of tension. Where before order and chaos had been contained, even rigidly differentiated, he could now feel the surge and beat of an older energy begin to thrive in the current of roots stretching beneath his feet. He felt stimulated and threatened in equal measure by the pace of this change.

The bamboo gave way easily and he gauged he was quarter of a mile or so from the shore when the sound of churning water became audible. The squawks and cries of animals and birds matched this commotion of roiled water as he drew nearer the raised banks leading down to the lake.

Scrambling through a thicket of oveida creepers he was suddenly loosened into a clearing of open ground with the sight of the lake before him. What he saw was like a cataclysm of energies and brutal defilements. The lake was white with the turmoil of disturbed water. A vast assortment of creatures lay one atop the other like compacted strata of rock. They were coupling, devouring and dying in a manner which signified that the normal boundaries of behaviour had broken down completely. Mammoth-like buffalo strove on the backs of huge fish, their penises plunging against flesh rather than penetrating. Birds, fish, boars, wolves, all sprang randomly at each other, either killing or perverting what they seized upon. The lake began to discolour with blood.

Little by little the frenzy died down. The creatures were exhausted, disorientated, wounded. Those that were able slowly made their way to the banks, the survivors shambling off to the forests north of the lake. As the waters settled and the light darkened to a burnt orange Hadge looked out upon the corpses floating or partly submerged and tried to fathom what impulse had initiated this horrible progression. Fearing for his own safety he began to make his way back towards the perimeter of the garden.

It was late afternoon when he finally heard the crunch of gravel beneath his feet and wearily he motivated himself to go to the east wing and examine Olan's condition.

—— ~ ——

In the week following her retrieval from the cage Olan recovered extraordinarily quickly, and without significant help from Hadge who was desperately trying to coax Liano out of her state of catatonic inertia. Initially he had thought that Olan would die and that the horrific frenzy of the animals was a prelude to this end. By the second day, however, her skin had cleared, its wrinkles smoothened out, its tone paling to a light cream so that it looked like alabaster. On the third day her eyes opened while her limbs discovered an old agility. She began to ask for clothes, perfumes and other oddments to be brought from her rooms. This revitalisation of her flesh and spirit was both dramatic and beautiful. Hadge was openly incredulous of this ability of hers to refashion herself so completely. She explained it simply as a concentration of the will, a channelling of energies.

By the fifth day he was convinced that she could harness enormous power and was increasingly intrigued by her. He had tried to engage her in conversation but she was dismissive of his inquiries and indicated that she would talk not at his urging but at her own discretion. Only once did she inquire about Liano and that was simply to ask what part of the Fortress she had retreated to. Hadge described Liano's condition in the hope that Olan might offer some advice but she appeared completely uninterested.

Even in these early stages Hadge could see that Olan had a dynamism, independence and beauty which he found compelling. A predatory sexual instinct began to stir in him as of old, one which he held in check by recalling his responsibilities to Liano and his unborn child. A doubt had arisen in his mind, however, as to whether the child would survive the trauma of this period. Liano had eaten little in these last days and a gauntness had begun to establish itself in her features. The thought occurred to him that he was beginning to give up on Liano, that she had in fact failed him. He found it difficult to remain in her presence, perhaps because he now felt that Liano viewed him as being immaterial to her survival. At some point he had decided that the balance of her mind would be restored privately and not by any action from without.

Day by day Olan became more beautiful. If anything she looked younger than Liano. She had a more compact, even nubile body, the kind which although he had denied it to Liano, he had always found most attractive. It was true that Liano had filled out but she could never fully disguise the streel of bones on which the fat hung listlessly. Throughout the pregnancy she had all the appeal of an over-ripe fruit. Hadge forced himself to stop and interrogate the nature of these comparisons and defamations. He knew that his failure to appreciate and be constant to Liano was unjust and something he was deeply ashamed of. However the need to be around Olan became stronger. He recognised the signs of his own infatuation but was helpless to stop it.

By the beginning of the second week Olan deemed it appropriate that Hadge's long awaited interview with her should be conducted.

On the day in question Hadge attended meticulously to his person, bathing in rosewater and dressing in a fine blue robe, one which Liano had made for him earlier that year. It was a deliciously crisp morning with the flowers and plants of the garden displaying exuberant good health. His head filled with a multiplicity of aromas as he walked from the north tower to her chambers.

Olan stood in front of the mirror. She felt her body and mind synchronised. Never before had she experienced such fluency in terms of her ideas and actions. After her long period of suffering she now believed herself to be invested with a new vision.

She was dressed in an array of bright colours simulating the plumage of the male buatu bird. Her hair was loose and flowed down over her breasts. Tiny wrist bells interleaved her movements with sound. She found herself mesmerised by her own transformation and the serene beatitude which she projected. As she seated herself cross-legged on the bed, there was a knock on the door.

Hadge entered. He had the slightly hectic air of someone in a state of high expectancy. However, the catalogue of questions he had formulated seemed to vanish as he passed into the room. When he saw her he was transfixed. He was immediately enthralled by the power of her presence and felt that finally he had sourced the mysterious and mystical root of Aganatz, the ultimate centre and authority of the Fortress.

She directed him to sit on a footstool in front of the bed. Though he tried, he could not remove his eyes from hers. They searched through to the pit of his being. With the tips of her fingers directed towards him he had the physical sensation of her moving through layers of skin, currents of blood, and of her fingers reaching in to the inner organs and massaging them in a manoeuvre which took something away from him. It was like a dissectional referencing of him, a peeling away, until he felt that she registered the essence of him. It was as though, in a short space of time, she came to know the secret of him, to know him in fact more rigorously, more honestly, than he knew himself. Everything about himself had been effortlessly betrayed and disclosed. He felt shame but also a tremendous sense of release. However, his impulse now was to try to guide her away, to shift the focus back onto her, to salvage some secret or to preserve a percentage of himself from her hands. It was useless. He was known and reduced by this transference of knowledge, and this relinquishment made him feel vulnerable, dependent. Summoning his will he tried to push her back, to lever her away and so regain his composure.

She recognised his effort and his fear and folded her hands. As he fixed his eyes on the window through which he could see the boughs of blago trees move restlessly in the wind, he heard her voice, at first dissonant and shrill, become gradually more mellifluous.

'You are Eighad's son. Do you know this?'

The words passed over him or hung contained in their own skein of sound. He believed he had the option to take them in his hands and hurl them back at her, or else draw them into his system and discover whether or not they could be measured as a truth. There was a terrible distortion and complexity in what she said. He could only deny it. But his voice trailed off and he was subsumed by his own reflections on all that had passed.

After a few moments she pressed him again.

'Who is your father? Tell me that.'

It was pointless. There was no answer.

'Are you my mother?'

'No. Better for you if I was. Your mother was the bitch Evina. Your father the bastard Eighad.'

His mind was like a vacuum, the room a cavity of darkness. He wanted to say something. He could say nothing.

Olan stretched out on the bed, the curve of her hips visible beneath the folds of cloth.

'Come,' she said. 'Lie down beside me.'

He lay down on the bed, face up to the ceiling, his body rigid with tension.

'Given time,' she said, 'I will answer all of your questions. All you want is an explanation but remember there is another context and words are not always sufficient. Hadge, you must have complete confidence in me. I know you now as no other. You must be true to me. Will you be true to me?'

'Liano is pregnant with my child.'

'Liano is your blood sister. The child an abberation. You owe her nothing as I owe her nothing. Look what she did to me.'

'Why? Why did she lock you up?'

'Liano has her own power but she is an evil reference. She is Eighad's child not mine. She lives aside from the rhythm of the garden. She is a reflection of her father, a corrugation of his hatred. It is his hatred of me that has made her behave in the way she does. So I forgive her. I bear her no malice.'

Hadge's mind felt ponderous, still he continued to question her.

'If Liano is that evil why has she retreated? Why does she sit in the same spot, barely eating, mindlessly repeating the same phrase. What is she afraid of?'

'She believes I have secured you. Have I? According to the rotation of good and evil, good is now supreme. Her actions are part of an inevitable sequence. You must not go near her. Let her die. Let the child die.'

'I cannot do that. Not now. If everything is as you say it is then I will have to verify it for myself.'

It took an extraordinary effort but Hadge rose from the bed and without turning back walked out of the room. He could hear her calling him but the words fractured and melted into the silence, distilled in his mind only by the angry tone with which they were pelted at him.

Once within the atmosphere of the garden he felt more isolated and alone. His mind swivelled on the same points, the same details. The legacy of his blood, his kinship to these people. What was right? Who was he to believe? The thought of leaving Aganatz came to mind but he knew he could not. He could never suppress what had passed here and his life would be a pointless migration without the truth. The truth. Phrases rang in his ears. Olan's words were turned over and over but they signified less and less to him as he tried to fix their truth or the application of that truth to his life. Everything appeared to have been enacted according to a pattern whose trace lines in the ground were too complex for him to fathom. He had to talk to Liano, to try to retrieve her, to understand.

The sun was beginning to fall behind the western battlements when he entered the ground floor quarters where Liano sat, still rocking to and fro. When she saw him she seemed terrified and the sound of her mantra filled the room. Hadge tried to touch her, to dissemble the threat she believed he posed. She scuttled away, her belly heaving. Seeing her like this he could only feel pity for her. The more he looked at her the less he could believe that she harboured the kind of antagonism Olan had described. He spoke to her gently, lovingly. But there was no response. Nothing in her eyes signified that his words had penetrated her consciousness. He left her for a while to prepare some food and then returned. Lighting a small candle he remained with her through the night. She ate some food guardedly, after having smelt and fingered it. By this one action Hadge felt the patience of his vigil rewarded.

For periods the incantation diminished to a low hum. Her eyes grew heavy and she lay down on the hard floor. As he moved to cover her with some blankets he saw a ripple of movement against her belly. A foetal kick. The baby was alive. He was exultant. He realised now that he wanted it more than anything else and was prepared to do anything to safeguard its life. It seemed irrelevant to him, the context of his blood relation to Liano. They had conceived a child together and he, for one, wanted to see it born. He wanted it desperately.

He lay beside her as she slept and was with her when she woke. Whether it was because of this sympathy of feeling or the fact that the fabric of her fear had shredded, he could not say, but as she stirred he sensed a difference in her.

'Liano,' he said, 'are you alright? Can you hear me?'

'Yes,' she replied. 'I can hear you.'

He moved to go near her.

'Stay where you are,' she demanded.

'What are you afraid of?'

She began to lapse back into the mantra.

'Stop it,' he screamed at her. 'Stop it. There's nothing to be afraid of. No one is going to hurt you.'

Suddenly she reared on him, her whole face animated by anger.

'You couldn't wait, could you. You couldn't wait until she was dead. Everything would have been alright. But no, you had to bring her out. Everything would have been alright.'

Her last phrase was more like a question, less of a reproach. Her eyes were vague.

'Liano, you didn't want to kill her. I know you didn't. Whatever happened is past. We can go on from here.'

'You know nothing Hadge. She has waited for this revolution of time. She has the means now for her revenge. I did not realise it until I saw her in your arms. She is planning to kill me and I know there is no escape. I know this as a certainty.'

'I am here. Is there nothing I can do?'

'You.' She seemed to reflect for a moment. 'You are lost to me. I can see it in your eyes. You too are dead.'

'No, Liano. All of this is beyond me but believe me I will not die, and neither will you. If you want we can go now. By my reckoning there are still four weeks to the birth. We can make it to Doan. Liano are you listening to me? We can make it to Doan.'

'No, Hadge you're wrong. We cannot leave.'

The silence which followed seemed only to enlarge this last statement and declare it as a truth.

'Hadge,' she said. 'Kiss me.'

The solicitation came from nowhere, was so completely unexpected that he was flummoxed. He knew that Liano had asked him to kiss her but he could do nothing. He could hear himself repeat over in his mind, Liano wants you to kiss her. This will serve as a reaffirmation of my love for her and a denial of Olan. Do it. For God's sake do it. But he couldn't. He could not move and he could not place his lips beside those of the creature on the floor.

Liano got up and walked out of the room. All she said as she passed was, 'Beware, Hadge. Beware.'

He remained in the room for the rest of the morning, mulling over the pattern of events of these last days, trying to see how the rhythm of hatred and fear could be broken, trying to find a kink or entrance into that rhythm which would allow him to effect some kind of rehabilitation. A state of tension oozed from every pore in the Fortress. Beyond the walls of the southern wing he could feel the battle lines being drawn and he visualised the two women arming themselves for combat. He felt ineffectual, girded by his own equivocation in the face of decisions he knew he would have to make at some point.

He saw Olan's power as a kind of mesmerism, an hypnotic presence manufacturing a state of attraction, a power which might ultimately subvert his will and make him over to her. He saw no other course for himself but to avoid her and attach himself in limpet fashion to Liano, whom he would protect as best he could if it came to the point where her life was threatened. As he thought of her now, he tried to reverse what had occurred earlier that morning. Recreating the scene he saw himself move towards her, bend and kiss her. But the kiss was never complete. He could not overcome, even in his imagination, an innate repulsion towards her.

By late morning huge clouds had swept down from the Kalakut range of mountains in the north and settling over the Fortress, the heavens opened. Thick pellets of rain showered down in a heavy torrent. The garden sapped this plentitude of moisture and Hadge could smell if not yet see, fresh growth rupture spontaneously upwards. The aroma reminded him of sex. It was a sour, sweet foetidness which rose from the soil. Rain filled the gutters and cascaded down the walls. When he looked out the window to the other wings they appeared as only vague semblances through the intense and persistent sheet of rain. The garden bore an uneasy silence. He had never heard it so quiet. He could make out animal forms underneath some ilb trees on the eastern perimeter of the great grass plain, but no birds sang. The only sound was the occasional squawk of a crested dogon bird.

Hadge tried to move out from his quarters but was pressed back by the rain. For seven days and seven nights it continued, an unrelenting downpour that caused the lake to overflow its banks and the irrigation channels, which fanned out from it, to sunder. After three days he was forced to move to the second floor. Seams and cracks appeared in the Fortress walls, with lumps of mortar and bricks being torn away to the point where the structure began to feel unstable. Going to an observation room two hundred feet above the garden he looked down. Water had submerged much of the plant life. Drowned animals floated on the surface while herds of the larger creatures had settled on high ground to the east and west. The swollen waters moved in dramatic currents around the inner walls of the Fortress, carrying with them debris, plants, and flotations of furniture, so that it seemed to Hadge that the innards of Aganatz had been flushed out and were trying to find a point of settlement in the murky depths of the garden.

At no stage did he catch sight of either Liano or Olan. They too he presumed had secreted themselves indoors and would remain hidden until the waters subsided.

The rains stopped as suddenly as they had begun and gradually the water seeped into the earth or was absorbed by the intense heat which followed. It was three days after this cessation that Hadge again ventured out into the garden. The ground was still sodden from the deluge and Hadge picked his way carefully over what was now a flattened mire. Those animals which had survived began slowly to reclaim old territories while the bloated carcasses of the drowned fouled in the heat. He knew that conditions were prime for the outbreak of disease and the sight of greater than usual numbers of vermin seemed to confirm this fear. Among the strewn carcasses he kept his eyes peeled for Liano. Lodged in his mind was the idea that she had been swept up by the rising waters and that behind some tree or hillock he would discover her barely distinguishable body. Sensing that events were beyond his control he began to prepare himself for the worst of eventualities. He could not discount the possibility that she had been killed by Olan.

Moving through a grove of tamarisk trees he heard a rustling in the undergrowth to his left. Something seemed to distinguish the movements as human and he called out.

'Liano. Is that you?'

Walking through a clump of bushes he heard the sound of feet at his back. A sudden fear gripped him. Turning he saw Olan standing under a laurel of green leaves. His first impression was that she was naked but as he looked at her he saw that two circularly scrolled discs covered her breasts, and that a triangle of black cloth over her pudenda was tied by a thong around her buttocks. Filaments of silver-like gauze gave an unusual aura to her flesh. In her hand she held Eighad's rib.

'Where did you get that?' he demanded. 'What have you done to Liano?'

Turning away from him, Olan began to walk through the grove of trees. Running after her he caught her and, grabbing her by the shoulders, swivelled her around. The very touch of her flesh shocked his blood and before he could suppress his instincts, his penis bolted against the fabric of his robe. Olan relaxed completely and melted her body against his.

'Don't be afraid,' she said. 'I've done nothing to Liano. How could I, when I know she means so much to you. The rib I found in Eighad's old room with the notebook he had with him when he died. Don't let go of me Hadge. Hold me.'

Turning her face up to him she said,

'Kiss me.'

Their lips met and Hadge knew that he wanted her with a deep sexual hunger which had to be sated.

Pushing him gently away she led him by the hand back towards the southern wing. As they walked she began to talk of Eighad. Her voice was passionately charged and he listened intently to every word.

'I cannot talk of Eighad without venting the hatred his memory summons up in me. Try to understand. Believe me when I tell you his violences were fastidious. He demeaned me so totally that I had no other wish for myself but to die. You have read his notebooks. You know something of his mind. What I am about to tell you is the truth and everything follows from this.

'After leaving your mother he travelled for some years in the north. On a journey south, by a caravan route to the east, he was told of the existence of the Fortress and of the woman who was believed to dwell within. He was intrigued and, leaving the caravan one night, he made his way across the desert to the great gates of the northern wing. For three days he remained outside, banging on the doors demanding to be let in. I was alone and up to that point I had had little or no contact with outsiders. I was determined to keep the gates barred against him. Gradually he wore me down. He was unarmed and promised to accede to any of my requests. I grew used to his presence and on the third day I lowered some food and water over the walls.

'I maintained him this way for seven weeks and would talk to him through a porthole in the gates. I began to trust him. I even felt that his absence, were he to leave, would be a great loss. It was something I didn't want to consider. I believe he understood this and at the end of seven weeks he asked for some supplies so that he could leave and make his way south. Almost immediately I opened the gates and from that day on I became puppet to his will and the focus of his abuse and violence.

'At first his manipulations of me were subtle, mischievous even. I had no experience with people and his words and actions were an authority to which I submitted. He declared his love for me, but it was a conditional love, a love synonymous with his decree that I existed for his empowerment. I had no value aside from him. Initially I was absorbed by him, by his attentions to me. His violence I recognised as a bond, one in which love and violence were synchronised, where they expressed a unity. In the end I could not separate one from the other.

'Whenever I began to make demands upon him, to try to alter the course of our relationship, to test whether a different habit of love would offer me more, he would threaten to leave. He would even carry out this threat, moving off into the desert for days at a time. But he was careful never to leave me long enough so that I could suspend my memory of him or disengage my heart. His returns only re-inforced my addiction to his violence, to his love.

'For four years it continued like this. For periods he would with-draw from me altogether, retreating to his room in the north turret, while I, feeling marginalised and rejected, connected myself inti-mately to the fabric of the garden.'

Olan looked to Hadge to confirm his attentiveness, pressured his hand and continued.

'By the end of that fourth year whatever balance had existed in Eighad up to then became distorted. He was increasingly manic, stalking me for days in the garden, setting traps, hanging dolls and masks from the limbs of trees, leaving the butchered genitalia of animals favoured by me on small stone altars, scrawling my name in blood on the walls. He believed he could only exorcise his devils through his defilement of me. He captured me finally among the blago trees, tied my arms to their limbs and my extended legs to stakes in the ground. He raped and sodomised me repeatedly. He used objects when his prick was no longer able to penetrate. My screams layered themselves into the bark. I killed him a thousand times and willed myself to remain alive so that I could revenge myself. When he cut me down, the ropes had burned through to the bone. He left me to die but not before offering me a final gesture of his disgust. Levering back his leg he slammed his boot into my groin and then into my face. I crawled to the pond and slid into the water expecting to sink to the bottom. Instead the lilies and fish kept me suspended and healed my wounds. I floated in the pool for days and when I was finally able to climb out, I had conceived of a plan to kill him.

'This terrible desire, this need to kill him was made more urgent when I realised I was pregnant. I wanted the child. I believed that I could deny his part in it, that I could make it over to me, that it would finally be something which was mine, a thing that would succour me in a way he never had. I believed I could extract him from my memory, that I could love the child as though it had been mine alone. As you see I could not. Liano was a continuation of him even though I showed her all the love a mother could. At the time though, I feared for my own life and that of my child.

'In the enactment of my plan I did two things. From large mirrors retrieved in the eastern wing I constructed angled reflectors and placed them in the desert according to a particular alignment. Painting my body with kohl, ochre and blood, I appeared to Eighad in as frightening a guise as possible. I offered him glimpses, a terrorising presentment managed by the hatred I felt for him in my heart. I watched him as closely as I could without betraying myself, trying to gauge the level of wariness I had induced in him. I tried to play on his own paranoia, to force him to leave and thus lead him into the centre of my trap.

'Eighad was a powerfully magicked person and I do not believe he was ever afraid of me but my actions registered with him at some point and he began to make preparations for his departure. All of these complex manoeuvres were necessary since I knew I could not kill him without throwing him into a momentary state of confusion.

'The mirrors, once set up, created a boundary, yet projected the illusion of infinite space. Once within the coordinates of that boundary his destiny was in my hands. On the day he left a great wind rose up from the north, drawing dust into the atmosphere, turning the sky an unearthly orange. I followed him for four days carrying with me the curved scimitar which would accomplish his death.

'There were times when I felt I could not wait for him to reach the designated spot. I felt so powerful that I did not believe he could stop me. However I knew him too well to risk such an action and remained behind. On the fourth day I began to close in. Where you discovered the grave was the point at which the reflections of the mirrors synchronised. Up to that point they had concealed my presence, now they multiplied it by three.

'Suddenly I was beside him, not as one but as a trinity of images. It was in that moment of confusion and terror that I moved the scimitar over his shoulders, lopping off his head. It was a moment of great efficiency, a moment of great beauty. I felt no shred of sorrow. I was released. He had underestimated me and this if anything was the only thing which saddened me. I dug a hole and kicked his body in. Kneeling in the grave I cut off his penis and ate it. As a final exorcism I slit his belly open and threw his guts about the floor of the grave. I believed then that I had rid myself of him forever. I was wrong. He still comes back at me. Sometimes I feel him seize me in the night, heaving over me, filling me with his vile essence. So you see Hadge, it is not over yet.'

Hadge looked at her. 'What will end it?'

'You Hadge. You will end it.'

They had come to the main entrance of the southern wing. Still leading him by the hand Olan took him through to the quarters he had renovated for Liano. Walking through the large drawing room which looked out onto the great plain they went into the bedroom where a huge oak bed lay flush against the whitewashed wall.

Sitting down on the edge of the bed Olan removed the silver gauze filaments, breast discs and thong. Naked she lay back and stretched out her arms. Hadge too had removed his robe and now fell upon her in a desperate frenzy, sucking her nipples until he felt what was like an electrical charge spark on his tongue. Grooved into the folds of her flesh he had the sense of returning to an old territory, an ancient movement of blood and sinew that was home.

Taking his penis in her hands she pulled back the foreskin, ran her tongue over the rearing head and gradually moved her lips down to the base. Her lips moulded themselves over his shaft and he could feel the tip hit the back of her throat. Groaning he emptied himself into her mouth. For a moment she seemed to gag but as she drew her head up from his groin he saw her throat move and she swallowed.

They lay in silence, then Olan gave the rib to Hadge. Stretching her legs apart he could see she was moist. Turning the rib around he moved the thicker of the two ends in slowly. It had hardly touched the rim of her vagina when she shuddered. Her whole body tremored. Although Hadge had a firm hold on the rib he could feel it being sucked into her. Her body jack-knifed suddenly and grabbing him around the neck with both arms, she began to thrust her bottom back and forth along the top of the bed. Hadge kept the rib firm, allowing her to maintain her own rhythm. She came again and again screaming Eighad's name with each climax. Hadge was terrified and aroused in equal measure. He wanted her to call his name. He wanted her to come to his name. Withdrawing the rib he pushed her back forcibly onto the bed, spread her legs apart and thrust into her. Now there was a terrible violence at the centre of the act and he drove into her with all his might. Olan wrapped her legs around his back and turned her face to the door. Standing in the doorway was Liano, her hand to her mouth, forcing herself to watch as Hadge climaxed in her mother. Olan looked at her and, with a smile Liano recognised from child-hood, emphasised her ultimate dominion over her.

There were tears in Liano's eyes as she turned away. Any vestige of hope that Hadge would remain true to her, an ally to whom she could have recourse when the time came, was now gone. Once again her mother had mustered her malicious will against her, had fouled the one good thing in her life. All she had left was the blossoming child in her belly, the substance of a precious ideal whose begetting might in the end salvage her. She would reclaim her life, her loving impulse, through the child. This was the only positive course she could envisage and she knew that to achieve this end she would have to kill her mother and Hadge.

When Hadge rose from the bed he felt soiled, as though he had taken part in a great travesty. Whatever personal morality he had ever espoused had been controverted by this act. He had denigrated not only himself but the bond he had made with Liano. His impulse was to go to her. Go to her now, he told himself. Tell her everything and ask her forgiveness. But what good would that do except loosen the guilt in his own heart and foster in Liano's mind an ever-deepening distrust as to the quality of his love. No, he must not tell her. The only solution was that his love for her should become a demonstrable thing. The birth was but a short time off and she would need him then. Everything would change for the better once the baby was born. The more he thought about it, the more it seemed that the baby was the means by which he could achieve a redemption of his relationship with Liano.

When he thought of Olan there was almost a palpable distillation of violence fluent in his blood. He knew that he had fucked her in violence, that the mental coruscations when he moved within her were vicious. There was no tendril of affection seeking to connect with something bountiful or beautiful. Still, it was a violence which held a terrible fascination for him. By attempting to deny it he merely established with greater force its apparent links to a creative power. In utter confusion he walked out into the garden.

There were rats everywhere. Carcasses of dead animals lay strewn over the plain with swarms of flies hovering overhead and mounds of beetles massed on rotting hides. The shadow of death lay over everything. The wind-blown stench when it filled his nostrils seemed to bring with it the larval bugs and maggots corrupting the decaying meat. He rubbed his arms in an effort to verify that his own flesh wasn't beginning to flake from his bones.

Shooing some vagrant carrion from one of the carcasses he examined it more closely. A vast range and density of insects were tearing off sections of bloated skin and squirming through the remnant intestines. Some of the bones had been picked clean so that their gleaned ivory caught the light of the midday sun. Even as he stood, ants and maggots crawled over his feet and began to work their pincers on moulting scales loose between his toes. Taking one of the fat cream bugs in his fingers he mashed it between his palms and spread its pulped life over his hands.

The flies, carrion and other tasters of death gave the garden a blueish hue. This was not the atmosphere into which a baby should be born but he could see no immediate remedy to the situation. In time the carcasses would be reduced to nothing, the vermin would resort to feeding on each other and some balance would be restored to the various sections of the garden. He had no idea how long this would take but felt that the safest course would be to ensconce Liano in one of the upper chambers, high enough to be free of the threat of rats and disease. There were enough supplies in the storerooms of the southern wing to cater to their needs. The main problem as he conceived it was to keep mother and daughter apart. He would meet with Olan once more and insist that she remain in the eastern wing. When a degree of normality had returned, then they could settle on the terms of a more permanent arrangement. With this plan formulated he went in search of Liano.

For the rest of the day he searched for her in every part of the Fortress but to no avail. At times he thought he caught glimpses of her only to find that she had vanished around the next corner. If she wanted to hide from him he knew it was well within her power to do so. Her knowledge of the wings was such that she could always avoid him.

At times he felt as though he was stalking her, picking up on hints and scents of her presence, following a trail like a primitive hunter, tracking her down. She was burdened by the weight of the baby, this in itself, he thought, would make her an easier quarry. The longer she avoided him the more it appeared to him that he was questing after a prize, trying to regain something he had lost, something which was rightfully his. He rationalised his movements as coinciding with his desire to safeguard the child. After all it was impossible to know what frame of mind Liano was in, impossible to know what injury she might do to herself. At times he had the feeling that he too was being watched, traced, harried to move on in this or that direction by a threat of shadows formulated at his back. After a fruitless search he returned to the southern wing to find Olan, but she too was gone.

As the days passed a great tension flexed itself in the structure of Aganatz. The very walls conjured up a muscled tautness. It was as if the foundations were held by a membranous skin which on the slightest relaxation would allow the veined stones to crumble to dust. Increasingly Hadge felt himself involved in a circuit of distrust and suspicion. He began to wait at vantage points, trying to gauge if he was being followed. An insidious paranoia enveloped him. If he could only see one or other of the women then he was sure the whole fiction would dissemble immediately. The fact of the rats and insects becoming more numerous only deepened his anxiety. He found he was afraid either to eat or sleep for fear of infection or that he would be ravaged. The rats had begun to colonise even the upper chambers. Nowhere seemed safe. All routes to the storerooms had been cut off and the exhaustion which now made his movements sluggish also induced a resurgence of the nightmarish reality he had experienced in the desert.

Hadge could no longer fathom the design of this chaos. At times he believed that Olan and Liano had killed each other and that the state of the garden emphasised the lack of a controlling hand. He had once conceived of the Fortress as a mass of brainlike channels. He wondered whether this level of disintegration reflected evidence of a diseased mind, a mind in the throes of complete mental collapse. Every natural sign presaged an end.

Earlier that day he had walked through the upper storey of the southern wing along corridors lined with glass cases containing aberrant creatures which had been sealed in, over what he suspected were millennia. The cases had been smashed and on the walls crept the hard-backed and flat-bottomed monsters, swivelling their antennae, grinding their jaws. Hundreds of them scuttled along the floors. He had heard screams of men and women, had seen lines of mutilated children stream through rooms, vanishing only to reappear again. He ran from all of this but the harrowing bondage of screams seemed to constrict his throat like a rope.

As time passed he came to avoid the interior of the Fortress altogether remaining instead on the high battlements where he continued to look down on the limitless gravel plain which stretched out beyond the circular fringe of dunes. It was four weeks since he had retrieved Olan from the chamber. The whole of Aganatz was in a state of utter chaos. His own physical and mental condition had degenerated. It was now that the desert seemed like a comfort zone. Its very sparseness beckoned him and he knew that if he was to survive he would have to try and get beyond the gates and make his way south. He stared blankly out into the middle distance and allowed the emptiness of the desert to fill his eyes. He had been looking at the same spot for some minutes before noticing the figure moving north north west.

Focusing his eyes he saw the form, draped in black, move onto the crest of dunes heading in the direction of Bradaz. There was something about the cloaked figure which described the presence of Liano. Running along the battlements he screamed out her name.

'Liano.'

The figure turned. It was her. He was sure of it.

'Wait. Liano wait for me!'

The figure turned again, walked down the far slope of sand and out of sight. He looked down on the garden below him where streams of vermin swept about the walls on all sides. Their mawkish squeals rose upwards in a drone of death. Girding his legs and arms with strips of moccasin and throwing a dark robe over his shoulders, he tried to blank out the sight of what lay before him. He made his way down the main stairwell of the northern turret. The noise of the rats filled his ears. When he stumbled he tried to protect his hands but it was useless. By the time he reached the main gravel path leading to the gates, his hands and arms were mutilated. Drawing the hood off his head he saw miraculously that the route ahead of him was clear. In the distance stood Olan. She looked beautiful and at ease. Immediately he wanted to attach himself to her, to ask for her protection. She beckoned him forward but when he reached the gates she was still beyond him.

'The door is open, Hadge. Go, I will wait for you.'

Seizing his chance he pulled the great door open. A blast of clean desert air filled his whole being. He looked down at his arms and hands. They were unmarked. He felt renewed. That was all that mattered.

Scrambling up the dunes which were now enveloped by the elongated shadow of Aganatz, he saw Liano about a mile ahead of him. He called her name but it was more in confirmation of her presence than as a direction for her to stop. For the next two hours he kept her in sight but was unable to gain on her. As they neared Bradaz, Hadge could see that the great rock had begun to fume, to pour out smoke and gases in a volatile combustion. The earth itself began to rupture and the tunnels Liano had once mentioned as extending from Aganatz, caved in, leaving a wheel of sinuous depressions. As the sky began to darken he lost sight of Liano amongst the ridges and defiles grooved upwards around the base of Bradaz.

'Liano,' he called. But the name hung in the air like a rattle of syllables released as an afterthought to life. As he climbed towards the flat area of ground in front of the cave, small rocks and movements of shale tumbled down. At any moment, he thought, Bradaz will spew its guts and bury us both. By the time he reached the cave, the foundations of the rock had begun to vibrate. He could almost feel its labouring mass swell towards the cratered top.

He had hardly entered this threatening density of shadows when he heard the lightest crunch of gravel at his back. Turning he saw Liano with a sword wielded lateral to his head and as far back as her distended belly would allow. Her face was impassioned, her pupils like maddened flecks in a sea of white. At that moment his life stopped. There was a split second visualisation of his death and, as a mental coda to it, his mind was trounced with a flow of images. Images of the rib, the square, the Fortress. He felt he had almost grasped the motif which summarised his course up to that point, when the sword began to move. Such was the intensity of the moment that the process was slowed. He could see the tiniest nicks and scratches on the curve of the blade as it followed through in a perfect arch. But there was a distortion, a kink in the fluency of Liano's action.

Their eyes met in the briefest of exchanges and he knew that she could not kill him. But that knowledge was in itself an afterthought to what occurred. The sword swept through under his chin grazing his throat. In an instinctive gesture he rushed to Liano in an effort to disarm her. They locked for a moment with the sword secreted between their bodies. A vibration of rock caused both to lose their footing and the sword moved like the direst secret into her heart. She fell on her side calling out his name, the life beginning to seep out of her. What were like spittle emissions of lava began to rain down around them.

Hadge knelt down beside her in a state of shock, his lips trembling, his eyes tearful, his whole being unable to credit what had occurred. Blood was now seeping from the corner of her mouth. She tried to say something. As he bent down an involuntary convulsion spewed his face with blood. Resting her hand on her belly she summoned what strength she had left.

'Hadge,' she said. 'Save the child.'

He hesitated. She grabbed his wrist and with a final effort said, 'Do it.'

Taking the hilt of the sword he drew it out of her body. His hands shook as he lifted the black robe over her stomach. Wiping the blade he rested its edge against the crease line below her navel and made a broad incision through the skin. She did not cry out. Cutting through the subcutaneous fat and muscle he disclosed the lower segment of the uterus. Liano had lost consciousness. He cut through the delicate membrane making sure not to go too deep for fear of marking the child. The baby's head presented itself and, moving his hands into the uterus, he lifted it out immediately. He cleaned its head of mucus and cleared its nose and mouth of waste. As he held it awkwardly in his hands it uttered a loud cry. A wave of emotion filled him and he drew the baby to his breast. The umbilical cord still trailed down, partly covered by the uterine sac. Tying it in a knot he cut off the excess with the sword.

Moving over to Liano, he checked for signs of life. She was dead. As he closed her eyes, initial flows of lava began to spew down. As a final gesture he bent and kissed her gently on the lips. Cradling the baby in his arms he made his way quickly down onto the desert floor.

He knew that he had no choice but to return to the Fortress. The thought filled him with dread but at the same time he felt empowered by the belief that all his energies were now directed towards maintaining the life of the child. With Olan's help they could find a temporary sanctuary in the garden until things stabilised. Given a few weeks the baby would be strong enough to make the journey south and they would leave Aganatz forever.

As he made his way over the final ridge leading to the Fortress he looked up to the battlements. He could see the figure of Olan like a great bird peering like an egret into the distance.

Olan watched him as he drew closer, the crinkled flesh of the new born baby visible in his arms. In her hand she held the sword with which she had killed Eighad. Its coolness shocked her blood, making the blade feel like a physical extension of her fingers. As they drew near to the gates she moved down onto the gravel path, her whole body organised to accomplish a death previously denied her.

The garden reeked of a terrible malfeasance and at that moment seemed to represent a reflection of her hate. Olan melted herself against stone and waited for the gate to creak open. It seemed like an interminable sentence of time. Then slowly the wooden gate moved inwards. Olan raised the sword. As Hadge entered, the gleaming rivet of steel slashed down on his skull splitting it in two. The curlicued segments of his brain reddened as the veins poured out their blood. He fell forward and lay face down in the dust. The child tumbled beyond him in a bond of cloth. Olan drew the sword out of Hadge's skull with an exultant scream.

Taking the baby in her arms she examined it and smiled. It was a girl. Stroking it gently she looked out on the desert and speaking to the wind or to a spiritual presence substantial in the wind, she whispered,

'Eighad. Can't you see. This is a new beginning.'